Randolph S. Foster, Louisa J. Crouch

Early Crowned

a memoir of Mary E. North

Randolph S. Foster, Louisa J. Crouch

Early Crowned
a memoir of Mary E. North

ISBN/EAN: 9783337270698

Printed in Europe, USA, Canada, Australia, Japan

Cover: Foto ©Andreas Hilbeck / pixelio.de

More available books at **www.hansebooks.com**

EARLY CROWNED:

A

MEMOIR OF MARY E. NORTH.

By LOUISA J. CROUCH.

Thou art gone home, O early crowned and blest!
Where could the love of that deep heart find rest
    With aught below?
Thou must have seen rich dream by dream decay,
All the bright rose-leaves drop from life away,
    Thrice blest to go!—HEMANS.

WITH AN INTRODUCTION

By REV. R. S. FOSTER, D.D.

NEW YORK:
CARLTON & LANAHAN.
CINCINNATI: HITCHCOCK & WALDEN.
SUNDAY-SCHOOL DEPARTMENT.

TO

MARY'S FRIENDS,

ESPECIALLY THOSE WHO HAVE AIDED IN THIS LABOR OF LOVE

BY

THEIR REMINISCENCES AND HER VALUED LETTERS,

This Little Volume

IS RESPECTFULLY DEDICATED.

INTRODUCTION.

THIS little volume is given to the public not because it is supposed to contain any special literary merit. It makes no pretension to this. Its chief claim is, that it is the truthful story of an uneventful, but noble young life: the faithful delineation of a *not* wonderful, but beautiful character. As a tribute of affection, designed to treasure up the memory of the dear departed, it is well understood that it will be most interesting to the large circle of personal friends by whom she was deeply loved; but the hope is cherished that it will be acceptable to others, and minister both pleasure and profit to them.

To pure-minded young readers, and to all such as are aspiring after the highest style of Christian life, it will not fail to be a winning and welcome voice.

Such as are content with mere worldliness—as have no sense of God—as, engrossed with the present, have no true ideas of the seriousness of being, no yearnings for goodness, for usefulness, for immortality—will find nothing here in their plans. Could they be persuaded to linger but a few hours amid these pages, pondering their simple but devout and deeply-spiritual teachings, they might perchance go hence bearing a wealth which they seek in vain in the more exciting volumes of thrilling but profitless fiction : lifted for the time above the stifling and intoxicating atmosphere of sense and folly, they might return to the common pursuits and perilous temptations of life with an inward power, the inspiration of superior truths, which would bear them, nobly and triumphantly, through all duty and trial, to that highest consummation, a glorious immortality.

It is impossible to behold a beautiful life, or even read of it, without feeling somewhat its exalting power. It becomes as a seed dropped into the soul, which fructifies and expands, transforming us. The communion works sympathy, and the sympathy culminates into a likeness. Souls are forever impressing each other, giving out good or evil according as they are. Blessed are the hours, and fraught with benedictions, that we spend in the fellowship of souls greatly good. It is like being on the mount with God.

There are two things, I think, in which the chief value of the book consists.

Primarily, in the insight which it furnishes into the growth and struggles of a youthful spirit in its passage from the image of the earthy into the image of the heavenly. In the letters which are so staple a part of the volume, and which give to it its greatest charm, we are able to trace the stages of development with perfect distinctness. Each in its turn marks an obvious advance. We behold the child-soul emerging, unfolding, expanding, taking upon it ever new and higher beauties, until at the close we are held in the admiration of a character all radiant with celestial light, vanishing away into a world of brightness.

The second noteworthy thing in the book is the light it sheds upon a Christian home. We are conscious all the time that we are mingling with a domestic scene lifted out of the common plane— that we are shut in with a class of influences peculiar and sacred. We are sojourning with a household in which God is honored, and the verities of the eternal and unseen world are potent.

But few of any age will be able to rise from the reading without feeling that they have for once found a home reared and conducted upon superior Christian principles—a home the antepast of the everlasting abode of the glorified. When shall Christians learn the secret here displayed? Daughters will not depart from the communion of these pages without being better, more dutiful, and helpful. Sisters will henceforth be truer, kinder, more loving; all will learn something of the spirit in which life's work of trial and useful labor is to be performed; will be more tender and considerate, more faithful and true, for having dwelt for even a few moments in the atmosphere of this sweet and loving spirit. No one will fail to see how religion exalts and beautifies life: how it sheds a halo over youth, and sustains and qualifies for all duty, bears up in all trial, and finally, being made perfect, swallows up death and life in a glory ineffable.

We are not of those who would inflict upon youth a mawkish and morbid pietism, robbing life of its pleasure. We would glorify it—fill it to the brim with the purest and loftiest joys—make the life that now is the beginning of the heaven that is to be. Youth ought to be buoyant and beautiful and blissful.

"Religion never was designed to make our pleasures less." They only have learned the true secret of happiness who have found their way to the "fountain opened in the house of David."

We knew the subject of this memoir well in all the vicissitudes of her brief life. We saw her in prosperity and adversity, and again in prosperity; when the flush of youthful health and beauty and hope was upon her cheek, and when, stricken by the hand of disease, she withdrew from the throng, to wait in the sick chamber her release from earth. In each case, the one as well as the other, she was happy. But few have had more to live for; none had a higher appreciation of life, a profounder enjoyment of all the beautiful and good there is upon earth. No heart ever more deeply loved the loving around her; but when she saw death coming, and felt that she must leave all so dear, looking up she beheld heaven open, and with shouting bade farewell to the earth, in the full faith that death was but gain.

How often it is ordered that bereavements follow in swift succession! During the time that these pages were in the course of preparation, death came a second time to the Christian home. The closing chapter recites the story of the sickness and death of Adolphus, the much-loved brother of Mary—a youth of rich promise, and exceeding beauty and maturity of Christian character. The one was scarcely glorified before the other was crowned.

A wise man long ago said, "Whom the gods love die early." We stop not now to inquire into the truth of the saying, nor yet to philosophize about it. Like most proverbs, it is possibly a half truth. In one view it is a mystery that anybody should die; in another, it is no less inexplicable that many should be permitted to live. The perplexity is double when those are taken away who give promise of a useful and happy life, while those remain to whom misery is appointed, and who accomplish no valuable end. In vain do we seek to understand the ways of Providence. It suffices that "He doeth all things well." When, as in these two cases, he calls away from homes of piety and love the young, the brave, the gifted, the beautiful, the good, there is a reason for it. Let us patiently wait. "What we know not now we shall know hereafter."

It will add interest to these memoirs, on the part of many readers, to know that the lovely Mary and noble Adolphus are the children of one with whom they have communed many times in the columns of almost all our Church journals, our highly esteemed and dearly beloved brother, C. C. North.

The thousands who have read with delight and profit his able articles, will breathe a prayer that he and his most estimable and deeply-bereaved wife may be supported under their great trial. Their honor is indeed greater than their sorrow. Blessed of the Lord are the parents who give to heaven such offspring. If need be, for a time there is sorrow ; but looking onward, the everlasting days are resplendent. Through the open door into which these glorified souls passed, we are permitted to behold a glimpse of the ineffable, which they henceforth gaze upon without intermission. "BLESSED ARE THE DEAD WHO DIE IN THE LORD."

PREFACE TO THE THIRD EDITION.

On a quiet hill-side in " Sleepy Hollow Cemetery," the neighborhood of which is made famous by the classic pen of Washington Irving, and not far from the spot where he is buried, now lie the remains of Mary and Adolphus North. There may be no such necessary connection between Irving's grave and the graves of these two young Christians as to prompt the mention of them together, yet to one who has read the life of each, and who has become familiar with the enchanting scenery where they sleep, it is but natural that they should suggest associations not wholly disconnected. Irving's fame was already commensurate with the English tongue when he died. His best monument is his books. But in the " Early Crowned " is seen the power of goodness to lift itself out of the comparatively narrow sphere of its creation and action, and to place itself in a position where it shall be widely and permanently felt. As in the case of the Dairyman's Daughter, a character was formed in domestic seclusion whose intensity could not be confined to the brief years and the limited locality of its formation, but must spread itself wherever moral beauty can be recognized and loved.

There is a deep interest attaching to every true life. The faithful delineation of the transitions through which an earnest soul passes, must always possess a charm so long as the feeling of a common nature binds all hearts in one. What we wish most in our reading, what does us most good, is to have *reality* so presented in its relation to the great principles which affect us as that we may see ourselves reflected in what we read. A biography which accomplishes this, though it embodies no startling facts, no novel opinions, and discloses no heart-rending crises, yet will never lose its freshness and usefulness. Nature perpetually sees itself in the mirror which a pure art holds to it.

Such has been the impression which the perusal of " Early Crowned " has produced upon its readers. In its first conception and issue it was hardly expected that it would attract attention much beyond the circle of the personal friends of its subjects; but it has been read far and near, and from all directions testimonies have been received both as to the pleasure it has awakened and the spiritual benefit it has conferred. Young souls have been converted, young Christians have been strengthened, and loving parents have been inspired by its pages. God has thus honored it so that the question of its continued publication is no longer one of gratification, but of religious duty. A third edition is called for, and is now sent forth with the prayer that wherever the simple portraiture of these young followers of Jesus may be read devout yearnings for the purest Christian discipleship may be begotten and nourished.

NEW YORK, *Jan.*, 1869.   H. B. RIDGAWAY.

EARLY CROWNED.

CHAPTER I.

INTRODUCTORY.

> These green hills thou didst so much love
> Yon river winding to the sea;
> The sunset light of autumn eves,
> Reflecting on the deep still floods
> Cloud, crimson sky, and trembling leaves
> Of rainbow tinted woods:
> These in our view shall henceforth take
> A tenderer meaning for thy sake;
> And all thou lov'dst of earth and sky
> Seem sacred to thy memory.—WHITTIER.

THE beauties of our noble Hudson have often been celebrated by both pen and pencil, and travelers from many lands have united in praising its surpassing loveliness. If it has ever been your privilege to journey in one of the floating palaces which are constantly passing to and fro upon its bosom, I doubt not you have been entranced by the charms of the scenery on either hand; but to study its

beauties more at leisure you must make your home
for days in some pleasant farm-house whose out-
look is river-ward, and at morning, noon, and night
watch its ceaseless flow, its ever-changing delights.

The Palisades, how grand! the chiseling of an
almighty sculptor; the hills, how freshly sweet in
their dewy grass and blossoming trees! the valleys
between, how tinted with sunshine and shadow,
the work of a divine artist! but more thoroughly
enjoyable are those hills whose summits are crowned
with pleasant homesteads, while down their sides
slope the fields of waving grain or fruit-laden trees;
the pleasant valleys, in which nestle the tiny cot-
tages of content; and the commanding eminence
with its grander mansion, showing by its situation,
as well as its decorations, that there abide some
who seek rest from honorable strife for competence,
in communion through nature with nature's God.
These speak of pleasant homes; of childhood happy
as the day is long; of youth more rationally spent
than in the whirl and dissipation of a city life; of
middle age enjoying pleasure in the midst of toil;
and of old age green and blooming, afar from tur-
moil, resting awhile in the land of Beulah ere sum-
moned to the celestial city. This is no imaginary
picture, for in the midst of these scenes lives the

family to which Mary belonged. Following a winding road from the Scarborough Station, we gradually ascend a hill until we reach the Vine-clad cottage so long the happy home of our most dearly loved.

Entering the little gate, and passing up the nar row side path, step on the verandah, and walking quite past the parlor windows, take your stand with me in the corner which overlooks the garden below. Mary's garden! the flowers still bloom, but she who planted them so long ago, and loved them so well, has gone where

> " Everlasting spring abides
> And never withering flowers."

What a scene is spread before us! Our path from the river has been gradually but steadily as-cending, and now as we look out upon the land-scape, bathed in the golden sunlight, we are ready to exclaim, " These are thy glorious works, Parent of good!" As far as the eye can reach, the river, like a stream of liquid silver, flows through scenes of beauty and transcendent loveliness. The blue hills on the further shore, the far away horizon of mingled sky and mountains, the nearer verdure of the "Point" and "Cove," make a picture seldom equaled; while in the foreground the flowery hill

side just below us, and the shady culvert, still
deeper in the dell, seem to invite us to search for
new beauties closer at hand.

In this lovely spot Mary spent three golden summers, and one quiet, happy winter. And though
she evinced much satisfaction when the mansion
was about to be built nearer the top of the hill,
and took much comfort in the thought of a
"homestead," a refuge for any of the family group
who, after battling with the world, should grow
weary, discouraged, or distressed, still she has often
said, "After all, perhaps we were happier in the
cottage than we shall ever be again, so cosy, so intimate, so sufficient for each other."

Leaving the "cot beside the hill," you will be
glad to stop the carriage, which is just passing,
and drive the rest of the way. The hill grows
steeper, and nearly upon its summit, above the
grass-grown terrace, the friendly door of "Ashridge" stands open to us.

If the scene below were beautiful, from here it
beggars description. From Mary's front windows
the landscape widens, opening new beauties to the
view; and as you gaze upon the sky, the water, the
earth, you cannot but think with Mary, that "If
earth were so lovely what must heaven be!".

> " But now, alas ! the place seems changed ;
> She is no longer here ;
> Part of the sunshine of the scene
> With her did disappear."

From this pleasant home one sunny day in August you might have seen a little company set forth with moistened eyes, subdued words, and quiet tread. The little ones after a season seem to forget their sorrow, and are almost merry as they journey toward the city; so happy are they with the presence of father, mother, and brothers all at once. But the silent tear in the mother's eye, the abstraction on the father's face, and the quietness of those usually joyous brothers, tell too plainly that an unusual errand is theirs. It is a holy pilgrimage to the grave of the first born on the anniversary of her natal day.

The first birthday Mary has spent in heaven ! How vividly and sweetly comes now to the family group the remembrance of former happy festivals, when some with pleasant gifts, and each with sincere love and good wishes, hailed the day so gladsome to them all !

> " God calls our loved ones, but we lose not wholly
> What he hath given ;
> They live on earth, in thought and deed, as truly
> As in his heaven."

Reaching the city and crossing the river, an hour or two finds them in Greenwood. Here must we leave them as they enter the inclosure where rests the clay casket which held their precious jewel. "Jesus wept" at the grave of one of his dearest friends, and surely to his followers the same blessed privilege should not be denied. This turf will be greener, and these flowers bloom more brightly, watered by tears of love, and tended by affection's hand, and we shall leave this last resting-place better and holier for communion with the sacred dead.

CHAPTER II.

HER CHILDHOOD.

. Thou hast no heavy thought or dream
    To cloud thy fearless eye :
Long be it thus ; life's early stream
    Should still reflect the sky.

Yet, ere the cares of life lie dim
    On thy young spirit's wings,
Now in thy morn forget not Him
    From whom each pure thought springs.
                                MRS. HEMANS.

MORE than twenty-one years ago, in the lovely flowery summer, was a little household blessed by the advent of the firstborn, a daughter. Many whose lives have been saddened by sorrow, have counted their years by winters; others, more moderate in their enjoyment of the good gifts of heaven, number their days by the springs; but to all who knew our Mary, it would seem most natural to say " for twenty summers she was with us," then

> " The light of her young life went down,
>   As sinks behind the hill
> The glory of a setting star,
>   Clear, suddenly, and still."

She was born in the city of New York, but the first years of infancy were spent in the South, till, in 1846, when Mary was but three years old, her parents returned to the metropolis.

As a child, there was little in her attractive to strangers, and few suspected the mines of hidden worth which were slumbering beneath that unassuming exterior. It was the work of education and grace to develop the resources of a mind like hers, and to transfuse in after years the beauty and purity of the heart through the external being.

Mary early developed a powerful will. When only two years old, she on one occasion was disobedient, and refusing to confess her fault, her father labored for hours to bring her will into subjection, when, at last yielding, she made ample confession, and ever after would obey her parents at a word.

Advancing in years, she was quite orderly and industrious, showing very early a taste for sewing, which never left her. When about six years of age, she was one afternoon seated in her little chair by her mother's side, busily sewing on some patchwork, when a visitor came in. The lady, as was natural, spoke to the little girl so industriously engaged, and wondered at seeing so young a child sewing so neatly. Shortly after, she sent to Mary a morocco needle-book. This little gift was accompanied by a note, saying it was " for the little girl who sewed so nicely, from one of mamma's friends." Mary took much delight in this, and used it for three or four years.

She was passionately fond of dolls, and until almost twelve years of age found pleasure in sewing for them and playing with them, enacting in miniature that motherly part which in after years was manifested toward her young brothers and sisters.

Among the qualities exhibited in early childhood was firmness and presence of mind. When, in their sports, her little brother would get hurt, without calling her mother, she would immediately run to the basin for water, and afterward to the closet for arnica.

Thus this little girl, in her fidelity and industry, exhibited a mind more sensible, solid, and discreet, than brilliant and fascinating; more remarkable for wisdom of conduct, than sprightliness of utterance.

The ordinary faults of childhood were hers, while selfishness greatly predominated. Of this she was always painfully aware, but lived long enough to have a naturally selfish character transformed into one of such marked unselfishness, that she became

pre-eminent for self-forgetfulness, and thoughtfulness of others.

When Mary reached the age of eight her parents
moved to the neighborhood of Manhattanville, a
few miles from the city. Here she spent three
pleasant years.

Here, doubtless, in the free, happy, out-of-door
life which the children led, was laid the foundation
of that robust and healthy development which
characterized Mary's young womanhood, and also
that love of nature which she ever after so strikingly evinced. In subsequent acquaintance with
her, how often, in speaking of the delights of a
country life, would she say, "I must tell you about
Manhattanville." Then with glowing face and
animated voice she would begin anew the story
we both loved so well: of the views from her windows, of the rambles of herself and brothers in the
woods, of their daily play on the lawn, and in the
orchard, and generally the narration would finish
with an account of the flower garden and her own
labor therein. She took much pleasure during
the first year of our school life in telling of that
happy time, and often as she concluded the recital would say, with a sigh which showed how intense was her longing, "I do hope that pa will

some day be able to have a nice country home of his own."

Mary's tastes were quiet. To her fondness for sewing was added a love of reading rather unusual in one so young. She seemed to prefer reading, or listening to the conversation of older persons, to talking herself. Always reticent, her friends were spared in her society that disagreeable infliction—a child who engrosses every subject of conversation which may be broached.

She did not begin attendance at school till twelve years old, at which period the family resumed their residence in the city, but received from a judicious and competent mother that elementary instruction, as well as the direction of that course of reading, which fitted her to enter at school into classes with those of the same age, or even older than herself.

If from the picture drawn of the child Mary, at work, at play, sewing, reading, or directing the little brothers, at this time three in number, you should fancy anything extraordinary, how have I misled you ! A healthy, active, plain looking girl, not particularly interesting or graceful, only conscientious and obedient, this is the daughter and sister as I would have you know her at this time.

Her parents still directing, guiding, giving "line upon line, precept upon precept," "bearing all things, hoping all things; but doubting not His word, "Whatsoever a man soweth, that shall he also reap," they sowed the seed of the word of God, and she has already reaped everlasting life.

O fainting mother, weary sister! whoever thou art that readest these pages, "be not faithless but believing." That same Saviour who, dying, remembered his mother, will remember you, and bless you in your labor of love, if so be that your faith fail not and your works abound.

> "In the elder days of art
>   Builders wrought with greatest care
> Each unseen and hidden part;
>   For the gods see everywhere.
>
> "Let us do our work as well,
>   Both the unseen and the seen;
> Make the house where God may dwell,
>   Beautiful, entire, and clean."

CHAPTER III.

BEGINNING THE CHRISTIAN LIFE.

Now I saw in my dream, that the highway which Christian was to go was fenced on either side with a wall, and that wall was called Salvation. Up this way therefore did burdened Christian run, but not without great difficulty, because of the load on his back.

He ran thus till he came to a place somewhat ascending; and upon that place stood a cross, and a little below, a sepulchre. So I saw in my dream that just as Christian came up with the cross his burden loosed from off his shoulders, and fell from off his back, and began to tumble, and so continued to do till it came to the mouth of the sepulchre, where it fell in, and I saw it no more.—PILGRIM'S PROGRESS.

We have seen how, among pleasant home sur roundings and Christian influences, our Mary's child-life was spent, but none save the all-seeing Father can declare the many prayers, the wrest-lings of spirit, the faithful labor of those devoted parents, who, not satisfied with dedicating their darling to God in infancy, still made it their duty and pleasure to guide her feet in the way of holiness. From her birth she had been guarded from every pernicious example and evil influence, and she had grown into a quiet, industrious, obedient child

The crisis in her life-history had now arrived, that gracious opportunity which comes to all, when childish things should no longer engross the immortal mind. Doubtless there are few at whose heart's inner door the Saviour has not knocked in early childhood; thrice happy they who, like Mary, open their hearts to receive the heavenly guest; they, like her, shall find his "yoke easy," and his "burden light."

At the age of fourteen Mary was a member of a Bible-class in her father's Sabbath-school. We know little of the exercises of her mind on the subject of religion previous to this time. During a season of increased religious interest in the Church, there was also renewed zeal on the part of teachers in the school. At an afternoon prayer-meeting held in the school-room, Mary, at the invitation of the superintendent, rose for prayers. Perhaps we cannot narrate this better than by giving her own words, written three years later:

"*August* 5, 1860.

"DEAR LOUISE: I suppose you will wonder why I should choose Sunday for writing to you. I thought I would write a letter different from any that I have ever written you, a purely religious one. . . . I have just come from beholding one of

God's beautiful sunsets. O how plainly is our Father manifested in his works! The sky was so clear, the heavens where the sun went down were a rich golden, increasing in splendor as the 'king of day' sunk lower and lower; it reminds me of the sun of life, when, as it gradually sets, the golden light and glory of heaven flood our souls. I would rather be a Christian in the most abject poverty, than a *princess* with 'no hope and without God in the world!'

You asked me some time ago to relate my conversion. I will do so now. Three years ago the first of February was Sunday, and pa had a prayer-meeting in the school. During the exercises he talked very seriously to the scholars, and finally gave an invitation for those to rise for prayers who felt an inclination to do so. One girl rose, and to my own astonishment I found myself on my feet. Of course it was the Holy Spirit made me rise. We went forward to the altar for prayer, and I felt very badly, and in the evening I went to church and sat in one of the side seats. When the invitation was given for those to go to the altar who felt sorry for their sins, I hesitated; but a dear friend who sat next me urged me to go, so I went. Several came and spoke to me, and toward the close of the meeting Mr. F., [the pastor,] Mr. L., and pa were all around me. I felt better, and when I came home I was on my knees praying for forgiveness till quite late. I lay down and soon my spirit grew calm. I went to sleep, and when I awoke the next morning I had a feeling of peace, and I started for school with a light and happy heart. So you see that I did not have any direct manifestation of God's forgiveness, but I was forgiven by degrees. Ever since then I have felt calm and peaceful, except at times I have been much depressed on account of sin."

A further extract from a letter written to a young friend about a month after Mary first started on a Christian pilgrimage, will be read with interest :

"*March* 6, 1857.

"Dear Addie: I have experienced religion, and am very happy. It is indeed a blessed thing to be one of God's children. I hope, Addie, that you feel the same as I do; if you do not, *do* seek to become one of his children, and pray earnestly that you may find, for you know the Bible says, ' They that seek me early shall find me.' "

Having taken this first step in the heavenly way, Mary immediately began to *work* in her Master's vineyard, and by precept and example, by consistent conversation and holy living, strove daily to lead others to the cross of Christ. Not only her own relatives, but also those young friends whom she so much loved, were entreated, persuaded, and prayed for by her. Two years after, in the spring of 1859, her three loved brothers, aged respectively fourteen, twelve, and nine years, were made happy in a Saviour's love, and joined the Church of which their dear sister had already been such an efficient member.

She takes occasion at this time, in writing to her cousin Annie, and her friend Addie, of this answer to her prayers, to press the subject of personal religion on each one of them:

"*March* 14, 1859.

"DEAR ANNIE: I want you to congratulate me. Charlie, Dolph, and Mason have been converted this winter, and I believe soundly. I think our family is one of the happiest on earth; we are all journeying toward heaven. We live in perfect harmony; our health, as a general thing, is very good, and taking all together, we desire to be no happier, except it be to live in the country, (our love for the country is by no means diminished.) I hope by this time, dear cousin, you have become a new child in Christ Jesus; if you have you are doubly dear to your loving cousin, MARY."

"*March* 17, 1859.

"DEAR ADDIE: I feel it my duty to assist ma as much as I can. I am the eldest of a family of eight children; surely a great responsibility rests upon me. My brothers and sisters look to me as a kind of second mother. I have to be very careful of my 'walk and conversation,' that I set them a godly and pure example in all things. I am happy to say that my three brothers have experienced religion this winter, and have joined the Church. I hope, Addie, by this time you are a child of God. If you are not, seek till you find."

Truly she worked while " it was called to-day." Young Christian, who readest this simple record of a life so well begun, so devoted ever after to the service of the Master, have you ever yet had the happiness of winning *one* soul to Christ? " He that winneth souls is wise," and you know not how many of your young acquaintance, knowing of your profession of religion, are waiting and longing for you to speak to them of those things which lie heavy on their hearts. They cannot open their minds to you; pride keeps them back;

but it is your duty to urge upon them the necessity of remembering "their Creator in the days of their youth." Your Master demands it, the Church expects it, and angels are waiting to rejoice over the sinner turned from the error of his ways through your instrumentality. The same Lord who has called you says, "Go, *work* to-day in my vineyard;" and if in this respect you follow Mary's example, great will be your reward.

And now, seeing how this earnest young disciple labored with a zeal and love, ah! too often wanting in many an older one, we can but notice how well she began to repay the love, the watchcare, and the prayers of her parents. It was on becoming a Christian that she awoke to a higher sense of her responsibility as the eldest daughter and sister; and never after did that feeling leave her, that she must watch over herself and the younger members of the family as one who "must give account;" that in all things she must be a pattern to them. Now she began to realize that

"We need not bid, for cloistered cell,
Our neighbors and our friends farewell;
The trivial round, the common task,
Will furnish all we ought to ask—
Room to deny ourselves—a road
To bring us daily nearer God."

I cannot forbear in this connection copying, as very appropriate, from an album given me when a child, a pen-and-ink sketch of which I have always thought Mary was the original:

"THE ELDEST DAUGHTER.

"She forms the connecting link which binds together both parts of the family circle—the parental and filial. Between the offended parent and the guilty but repentant child, she becomes the mediator; and oft, by her sisterly importunings, does offended authority find excuse for withholding the exercise of its power. She is the oracle of all the little troop, her sayings and doings forming in their estimate the measure of duty. How doth her gentleness smooth the roughness of her romping brothers, and distill the spirit of submission into their willful hearts! How do her example and discreet words exalt and strengthen those gleeful sisters, who lay at her feet the praise or blame of their conduct! If to her natural amiability be added the sweet influence of a Christian character, then indeed may she become the wise exemplar to her brothers and sisters, and a principal reliance to her parents in guiding the family group to heaven!"

Besides laboring for the good of others in the
family and social circle, she, when but sixteen
years old, took charge of a class of little boys in
the Sabbath-school. On assuming the responsibilities of that position, she resolved to be an
exemplary teacher. Always punctual, always spiritual, with lessons always prepared, she seemed
fully determined to improve the time. From a
journal which she began at this period, we can
obtain a glimpse of her inner life, truly " hid with
Christ in God."

" *Jan.* 7, 1860. —The first week in the new year is
fast drawing to a close, and soon we'll sing ' another
six days' work is done, another Sabbath is begun.'
I have never kept a diary previous to this present
time, but I resolved to keep a record of my feel-
-ings, experiences, etc., at the beginning of this
year. New-Year's day came on Sunday. I did
not commence this diary then, and have put it off
until the present time. I am the oldest child of a
large family, and I feel that a great responsibility
rests on me; am I adequate for the task? Of myself I am nothing, but through Him who loved me
I shall be able to perform it. My brothers and
sisters look up to me, and how careful I ought to
be of my example. O that I could lead such a

life as would be productive of good here on earth, and win for me a crown of life! I was about fourteen when the Lord had mercy upon me; he took a wandering lamb and brought it safe within the fold. Would that it might always stay there!

"It is now Saturday night, the close of the first week of the new year. I wonder if I have lived any more like a Christian should live than I did the week before. I come far short of my duty; I know that I have not lived as I should. I have set out this year with the determination to live a more holy and acceptable life before God, but I cannot do this of myself. He hath said, 'My grace is sufficient for thee.' Blessed assurance! I feel that I shall be able to live more like Christ. O holy Father, aid me! Thou knowest my weakness. Thou knowest my frame, and rememberest that I am but dust. O give me strength and grace to overcome temptation! When temptation assails me, I am so ready to yield; but remembering the promise that thou art a very present help in times of need, I shall be able to overcome. O Lord, how exceeding great are all my blessings! Thou dost shower thy mercies with a liberal hand upon me. How undeserving I am of even the least of them. What an ungrateful wretch I am, and yet thou dost bear with me. 'Slow to anger and plenteous in mercy' art thou. 'What shall I render unto the Lord for all his goodness to me? I will take the cup of salvation and call upon his holy name.' O my God, help me this year to live just as I should, like a true Christian. Help me to be more like my blessed Master, to live more and more like him. Help me to love thee more, and serve thee better; to glorify thy holy name in all that I do and say; and may my example be such a one, that others seeing it may follow me as I follow Christ. O my precious Saviour, how I love thee! how infinite is thy love for me! When I think of thee sitting at the right hand of the Father, and pleading for me, can it be possible that thou doest this for *me*? Yet I know that it is so. When I think thus of thee I scarcely know where to put my head. I feel to-night that I could be a great deal better than I am. I trust God smiles upon me, and lifts upon me the light of his countenance. I have never yet been fully satisfied of my acceptance with God, yet I have a humble hope that God has graciously pardoned all my sins.

"Another thing that I intend to do this year is to read my Bible, study it more, and follow its blessed precepts. I must close for to-night.

"*Monday, Jan.* 9. Yesterday I went to Sunday-school twice, but did not attend public worship on account of circumstances at home. I am a Sunday-school teacher, and have under my charge eight little boys to train for heaven. I have not had a class long, only a few months. My scholars are very restless, full of fun and mischief. I sometimes almost get discouraged, but the thought that perhaps if I give up this class some of the little ones will be lost, spurs me on. I need thine aid, O Father, in training these immortal souls! My little ones love me, and I love them. I have been trying by God's help to do my duty, and I think that I succeeded pretty well yesterday. I passed a very comfortable day. How pleasant it is to ' dwell in the courts of the Lord's house.' ' I would rather be a doorkeeper in the house of my God, than to dwell in the tents of wickedness; ' thus saith the sweet singer of Israel, to which my heart responds amen.

" To-day I went to school, passed my time there very pleasantly and I trust profitably. I worked out a sum in Algebra, which gave me a clear conception of a principle that I had not known before. I always feel so glad when I come out victor over a sum.

"I have passed a peaceful day; nothing very remarkable has occurred. One of my greatest troubles is secret sin. I can say with David, 'Search me, O God, and see whether there be any evil way in me.' 'Cleanse thou me from secret faults.' O! can I ever be a perfect character, and live without sin? It is so hard to do what is right and well-pleasing in the sight of God. O Lord, keep me under the shadow of thy wing this night!

" *Saturday, Jan.* 14.—It is some nights since I have written in you, dear journal, and during that time many circumstances have occurred. I have a great taste for reading, and when once interested in a book I let other duties go for the sake of reading. Thursday afternoon I was reading a book called the 'Pillar of Fire,' and was so interested that I neglected my duties; the consequence was condemnation. O when can I ever learn to do well! On Friday I went to school, and in the afternoon attended class-meeting. Our class is composed of young folks out of the Sunday-school. It originally consisted of a few girls from twelve to fourteen years of age. This little band was like leaven, leavening the whole lump. God graciously visited our school, and added large numbers to our class,

so that we numbered about seventy-five. We used
to have delightful meetings, and God indeed remembered his lambs. After a season it was found
necessary to divide the class, and one part met on
Sunday and the other on Friday. I belong to the
latter division. Pa is the leader of the class, but
not being able to attend to-day, Mr. L. led in his
stead. What an excellent leader he is! I was
very much impressed with one remark that he
made. 'Always say what you mean, and mean
what you say.' I think that it is an excellent
motto, and with divine aid I will try and practice
it. While in class I felt very much dissatisfied
with myself. I was thinking about myself when
these words were sung:

> 'This all my hope and all my plea,
> For me the Saviour died.'

Yes, thought I, 'for me the Saviour died,' and the
tears came rushing to my eyes, and I felt indeed
that this was my only plea. And O what comfort it gives me! of myself I am nothing, but the
Saviour came down to earth, and suffered death
for every man. 'God so loved the world that he
gave his only begotten Son, that whosoever believ
eth on him should not perish, but have everlasting
life.' O Lord, on this Saturday night, bless me.

Remove the stains of sin from my heart. 1 want not only the sin, but its stain washed away.

> ' My crimes are great, but don't surpass
> The power and glory of thy grace.'

' Come now and let us reason together, saith the Lord : though your sins be as scarlet, they shall be white as snow; though they be red like crimson, they shall be as wool.' O blessed promise ! Blessed be thy name! though my sins be as scarlet they shall be white as snow. Heavenly Father, give me grace to go through with my duties to-morrow, and grant that some word may fall from my lips which shall produce abundant fruit.

" *Sunday Evening, Jan.* 15.—This morning I went to Sunday-school, and I think that I fulfilled my duties as a teacher faithfully. My class was not as full as usual, probably owing to the bad walking. I think there is quite an improvement in the conduct of my boys. They seem to take more interest in the lessons, and obey me better. I do not let them read out of the Bible for their regular lesson, but I have a book given me by dear Aunt Emeline, called ' Line upon Line.' It is a most excellent little work; it gives an account of the creation, the history of Joseph, Moses, etc., and the story is more connected than in the Bible.

The boys seem to take quite an interest in it. I
read about Rahab and the spies to-day, and they
seemed quite attentive, at least some of them.
They have catechism lessons also.

"To-day is the eleventh anniversary of the dedi-
cation of our church, and several of the former
pastors were present. Mr. F. preached this morning; his theme was the ' Vine and its branches.'
He described the vine and its branches, some bearing fruit and some withered. Some branches bear
more conspicuous fruit than others. While the
fruit on the outside of the vine showed very
plainly, yet that underneath, in the shade, was just
as luscious and good as the more conspicuous.

"While ministers and official men were more
conspicuous, some poor member of the Church
bore just as much fruit to the glory of God. He
said also that the great Vine-dresser thought it
necessary to prune the branches, and while he
reluctantly made them bleed, yet it was for their
good, and that they might bring forth fruit more
abundantly."

Mary always had doubts about the expediency
of keeping a journal as a record of personal experience, so she discontinued it, but she wrote much

to her young friends, as well as to her relatives at a distance. She was an indefatigable correspondent, seeming to take much delight in sharing her pleasure with her friends in this manner, as well as sympathizing with them in their griefs. From a letter written in August, 1860, about six months after she discontinued her journal, we read the following:

"My heavenly Father knows that I love him, and that I want to do all I can for his cause. But it is such a cross for me to speak in public. Pa has a meeting in a schoolhouse near by, and I am so afraid he will ask us to speak that it worries me. I pray for strength that I may confess Him whom I love, but it must be that I do not pray in faith. Is it not strange that we will sin when we know that we are losing our happiness here and hereafter by so doing? O that the 'great and notable day of the Lord would come,' when 'all the earth shall know him, from the least to the greatest!'"

It was in the autumn of 1860 that Mary was transferred in the Sabbath-school from her class of boys, to take charge of one of girls about twelve years old. My own class was seated directly behind hers, and I remember well the appearance of those youthful heads all clustered together, while the eloquent face of the teacher, and the interested looks and tearful eyes of the scholars, plainly told that the low tones of Mary's voice were pleading with them, by every sacred consideration, to devote themselves in their *youth* to their Saviour's service.

Feeling so deeply the burden of souls, she visited each at home, relieving those found in destitute circumstances, and endeavoring to interest the other members of their families in religious things. Not considering her duty done when she had taught them, and relieved their temporal necessities, their seperate cases were carried in prayer to a throne of grace. She exhorted them individually in the Sunday-school class, sat with them in the evening meetings, accompanied them to the altar for prayer, till nearly all of them were converted, and became consistent members of the Church.

Resuming after so long a time the entries in her journal, she writes thus of her labors in Sunday-school:

"I sometimes think that I accomplish little or no good; but I feel that I have done something this winter. Five of my beloved scholars have been hopefully converted to God. I have but one scholar now who is not a Christian. O! thanks be unto God who hath wrought marvelous works in our midst."

These scholars ever retained their love and gratitude to their faithful teacher for her instructions and prayers in their behalf. May they all meet her in heaven!

Another extract from her journal will show how, though her labors were so abundantly blessed, she still was as "a little child" before her heavenly Father.

" *Sunday, May* 12, 1861.—It is a lovely Sabbath afternoon. The air is mild and balmy; all is quiet around me, and my own heart is full of praise and thanksgiving to my Father. I was permitted to partake of the sacred emblems of my Saviour's precious body and blood this afternoon. I can hardly pen my thoughts and feelings.

> ' Alas, and did my Saviour bleed?
> And did my Sovereign die?
> Would he devote that sacred head
> For such a worm as I?'

Thou wast bruised for my transgressions, and wounded for my iniquities. Thou didst suffer everything for me. O my Saviour, can I ever find language to thank thee! Grant me thine aid to glorify thy holy name by my life. I am so unworthy of the least of thy mercies. My soul is sometimes so overwhelmed with a sense of my own unworthiness, that I am almost discouraged; I am ready to sink. The 'horrors of hell' get hold of me; the sins of my life rise up against me, and present such an array that I am confounded. But 'why art thou cast down, O my soul, and why art thou disquieted within me? Hope thou in God, for I shall yet praise him who is the light of my countenance.'

"My soul trusts in the Lord this afternoon. I am deeply sensible of my ingratitude, my unworthiness; but still in the midst of all this I can exclaim, 'The blood of Jesus Christ cleanseth from all unrighteousness!' Thanks be unto God who giveth us the victory, through Jesus Christ our Lord.

"My greatest troubles are my secret sins. O how deeply do I deplore my wicked passions! All is not yet subject to the law of Christ. May patience have her perfect work in my heart, so that I may be perfect and entire, wanting nothing. My first impulse, when anything crosses my will, is to take some revenge: for instance, if one of my brothers, or sisters, or parents, cross or vex me, I want to strike, or vent my feelings in some wicked way. O how I have to struggle against my natural feelings, how much of grace it requires to overcome! Alas! too often do I yield; but, by the grace of God, I am determined to overcome and overcome, until I conquer fully and wholly every evil passion."

With two more letters, every line of which is full of her love to God and her friend, we must close this chapter of Mary's early religious life.

"*June* 5, 1861.

"MY DEAR FRIEND: I should feel far better pleased if you were numbered among the 'household of faith.' It is dreadful to think that you are an enemy of your Saviour; why don't you seek him? You are old enough to feel your need of him, for you have said so. He is far more willing to receive you than you are to go to him. He has left some most precious promises for those who are willing to forsake their sins and turn unto him. He says, 'Though your sins be as scarlet, they shall be as wool.' If you were numbered among the children of God, you would feel such a sensation of security, and then you would feel so strengthened for the performance of your duties,

and you would have aid to govern and control
your temper. Of yourself you can do nothing,
but through Christ you can do all things.   It is
not necessary that you should go up to the altar
in the church, in order to become a Christian ; you
can just as well feel God's presence in your closet
as in any public place.   Now, dear friend, do seek
the Saviour.   He will fully and freely pardon your
manifold sins, if you but seek him with your whole
heart; go and throw yourself at his feet, and confess all your sins.   After having confessed them,
then forsake them never to return to them again.
Try, Addie, and may God in mercy bless you and
keep you safe beneath the shadow of his wings.
Let the language of your heart be,

> ' Jesus, lover of my soul,
> Let me to thy bosom fly.'

"If you are in doubt upon any point, write and
freely tell me, and I will try to help you the best
that I can."

"*July* 24, 1861.

"DEAR FRIEND: . . . It *is* wonderful how the
grace of God can sustain a Christian in his dying
hours. . . . In speaking of your feelings you say
that you feel that you 'are a great sinner, the chief

among a thousand, but you have not the power to
become one of God's children.' Now here you
are in error; of your own self you are incapable of
doing anything; but, through Christ strengthening
you, you can do all things. You certainly have a
desire to become a child of God. Have you not
the *will* to become a Christian? And why not give
up your will to his and say

> 'Here, Lord, I give myself away,
> 'Tis all that I can do!'

> 'This all my hope and all my plea,
> For *me* the Saviour died.

> 'I the chief of sinners am,
> But Jesus died for me."

"O, Addie, give yourself up to the Lord; he is
so full of mercy and goodness, and he yearns to
fold you to his bosom. Angels watch the struggle
that is going on in your heart, with trembling, and
O! why will you not let the right prevail? And
with what joy would the angels tune their harps
and sing praises to God over another repentant
sinner! I would I could make you one of the
Lamb's chosen ones; but I can only counsel and
pray for you; it all rests with yourself. God grant
that you may do right. Once more I beg of you,
give up your heart, will, and everything to God,

4

and O ! beware how you grieve the Holy Spirit by continually hardening your heart against his blessed influence. You know that the unpardonable sin is to steel your heart against the Holy Spirit, till, finally, grieved and saddened, he leaves you never to return.

"O come to Christ! 'The Spirit and the bride say, Come. And let him that heareth say, Come. And let him that is athirst come. And whosoever will, let him take the water of life freely.'"

CHAPTER IV.

AT SCHOOL.

Maiden! with the meek, brown eyes,
In whose orbs a shadow lies,
Like the dusk in evening skies!

Standing with reluctant feet,
Where the brook and river meet,
Womanhood and childhood fleet!

O thou child of many prayers!
Life hath quicksands, life hath snares;
Care and age come unawares!—LONGFELLOW.

WE have thus far taken a glimpse of Mary's life as of one forgetting not "to do good and to communicate;" we have now the pleasant task of watching her student life, as she received instruction from those who first loved and then admired her.

Her school life proper began in 1857, at the Van Norman Institute, where she remained four years. Here she soon gained the esteem of both teachers and schoolmates, by her conscientious attention to study, and kindness to any who seemed in difficulty. Her instructors all speak of

her in terms of highest praise; not so much for
the brilliancy of her performances, as for the pains
bestowed on all her studies. The principal of
the school, Dr. Van Norman, has thus written his
estimate of her character as a young Christian at
school:

"Mary having, before commencing her studies
with me, chosen the Rock of Ages for the foundation of her spiritual character, was thus prepared
to lay deep and strong the foundation of her intellectual life. She had taken Christ for her portion;
and in the Cross she had found both an argument
to show the vanity of the world, and a power to
overcome and displace it. In Christ she found
abundant resources for every trial and emergency
of her school life.

"She commenced with an earnest plan of life, a
plan having in it a principle, aim, and method, and
most successful was she in carrying out her plan,
because she took it to the foot of the Cross, and
sheltered her weakness under the strength of the
Omnipotent.

"Hers was not the imitative study of attitudes
and graces, but an earnest search for truth, and
the springs of a pure and beautiful life. Her entire
school life was a practical answer to Schiller's in-

quiry, as well as an illustration of the truth he taught:

'Doth the harmony
In the sweet lute-strings, belong
To the purchaser who, dull of ear, doth keep
The instrument? True, she hath bought the right
To strike it into fragments; but no art
To wake its silvery tones, and melt with bliss
Of thrilling song! *Truth* for the *wise* exists,'
And *beauty* for the *feeling* heart.'

"In scholarship Mary was thorough. Never satisfied with a superficial knowledge of any subject in the course of her studies, she patiently and perseveringly grappled with difficulties till they were overcome. Thus her intellectual growth was steady and vigorous. It was a daily joy to meet her in the class-room; for she manifestly had a high and dignified purpose in her school life. She needed no paltry motives to laborious application; love to God and parents was in her heart a perpetual fountain of pure, lofty, and effective inspiration.

"As might be anticipated from this character of mind, Mary was remarkably, I may say, for one of her age, peculiarly thoughtful and circumspect in her conversation. With this characteristic so strikingly prominent, all her teachers were especially impressed. One of them, who had spent many years in schools for young ladies, once said to the principal, 'Miss N. is the most exemplary girl in conversation I ever knew. I have observed that in the recesses she never engages in the ordinary gossip of her companions, but is always either studying, or talking on some profitable subject.'

"I believe that during the whole period of Mary's connection with my school, she was not known to speak one word of aspersion or detraction. On the contrary, it was remarked by all that she was ever ready with the mantle of charity to cover the faults of others. 'In her tongue was the law of kindness.' She was thoroughly imbued with the spirit of Christ, as wrought out and exemplified in the character and life of the excellent Caroline Fry, who, in giving counsel on this subject, said, 'Consider the dangers, the sorrows that lie in the path of all to their eternal home, the secret pangs, the untold agonies, the hidden wrongs. Thus the heart will grow soft with pity toward our kind. How can I tell what that censured person suffers? That fault will cost dear enough without my aid. So you will fear by a harsh word to add to that which is too much already, as you would shrink from putting your finger into a fresh wound.'

"Another strongly marked and impressive trait

in Mary's character, as developed in school, was a conscientious adherence to her convictions of right and duty. This indeed was the foundation as well as the crowning glory of her singularly pure and excellent life. Never did she in questions of duty ' confer with flesh and blood.' Her only inquiry was, ' What is the will of God ? ' A conflict seemed to her sometimes to arise between the claims of home and the demands of school. Often did she in these controversies, carried on in her own mind, confer with the principal, when, with the overflowing love of a daughter and sister, she would inquire, ' Is not the sacrifice made by my dear parents for my education too great? Mother is not in good health, and I feel that she needs all my time and energies at home.' From these conflicts she always came forth nerved with a stronger purpose to turn to the most effective account all her moments and opportunities at school.

" She deeply felt the responsibility involved in her relation to the home circle as the first-born, the eldest sister, and she longed for the coming time when, with suitable preparation, she could devote herself to the work of aiding her parents in the care and right education of her brothers and sisters. A spectacle for the admiration of angels

were the filial and sisterly affections and sentiments
of this young Christian as manifested in her school
life.

"Nor would the portraiture of Mary's character
as pupil be complete without reference to other
qualities, which, in striking contrast with the affect-
ation, prudery, and coquetry so prevalent in our
day, invested her with a peculiar charm.

"Simplicity, sincerity, purity formed for her a
triple robe of rare loveliness, and secured for her
the most solid and valuable friendship. All who
knew her well, agree that she possessed these vir-
tues in a very eminent degree. To her pure mind,
all things save sin were pure. This purity of
character led her naturally and easily along the
straight and even path of guileless sincerity, upon
which ever rests the sunlight of heaven.

"Such was Mary at school; and such are the
precious memories of her school life—memories
which, like angel voices, shall pour melody all along
life's pilgrimage quite to the gate of heaven, then
mingle with the joys, and swell the songs of
Paradise."

As a fitting accompaniment to this affectionate
tribute of our beloved teacher, perhaps I cannot
do better than to insert here a few lines written,

since our beloved one left us, by a school friend, whose acquaintance, there begun, soon ripened into enduring friendship. Augusta writes :

"My two years' friendship with Mary at school seems very short to look back upon now, with the thought that it can never be renewed; it was long enough to make me respect and love her. Her peaceful, happy death was a fitting end to her consistently beautiful life. She seemed to me when we were at Dr. V. N.'s the most really religious girl there. Her aim in life was at once the simplest and the highest, to be good, to 'redeem the time,' with an eye single, and a purity of heart I have never seen excelled."

My own recollections of that happy school-girl time are indelibly associated with Mary. First made acquainted through Church membership and mutual Sabbath-school interest, (though our parents had been friends long before;) our situations at home as eldest daughters so similar, our ages and tastes so much alike; in the intimacies of daily school life so closely knit together; our homes so near that the long walk to and from school was always taken in each other's company, and our classes and studies so generally the same that all our interests were common. How we enjoyed

those walks, and the long time for conversation
which they afforded! The first topic would very
naturally be the preparation of the day's studies,
and an argument perhaps on some subject or
opinion advanced or asserted by a particular author.
From this starting point we generally wandered to
things possible and impossible, more than any one
except school girls had ever dreamed of. Mary's
conversation was always free from those two topics,
alas! so common to young ladies, "dress" and
"other folks." I remember at our first acquaintance with what admiration I regarded this trait in
her character, deepening as I discovered it to be a
fixed principle to have her conversation "profitable." One instance in particular I now recall.
Our attention was attracted one fine morning in
early spring to an unusually bright display in a
store window which we were passing. I said,
"Mary, do you think much about your change of
dress as the seasons come round?" And with a
simplicity and *naivete* peculiarly her own, she replied, "O yes, I think about it a good deal, but it
is not worth while to talk about it any more than
you can help, is it?" She would frequently in our
conversations say how much greater were our advantages than those our parents had enjoyed, and

that the only way in which daughters could repay
the toil and care they cost father and mother was
by being so diligent and industrious as to show
that their kindness was appreciated. Then our
talk would sometimes glide into other channels of
efforts to do right and conquer the sin within us;
Mary always speaking with much humility of her
own short-comings and feeble endeavors to do
good.

I have somewhere read a passage like this:
"As the great apostle Paul grew in grace he became more humble; when his heart was first
melted by the grace of God, and filled with holy
love and zeal, he said, 'I am not worthy to be
called an apostle;' when his labors had been abundant, and his sufferings for the cause of Christ
severe, he called himself 'the least of all saints;'
and after he had 'fought a good fight and kept the
faith,' he styles himself the 'chief of sinners.'"

Such seemed, to all who knew her, to be Mary's
estimate of her own character. Never having a
high opinion of herself, or her own attainments or
usefulness, she daily grew less self-confident and
more humble, and on her dying bed, receiving a
letter from a friend who thanked her for the good
she had done, Mary raising herself said, "What

good have I done her, mother? She has always been good to me, and I have done so little for anybody." O Mary, friend, thine unconscious influence for God and holiness is not the least of the good thou hast done! Looking back upon those happy days I cannot but feel that

> "The head which, like a staff, was one
> For mine to lean and rest upon ;
> The strongest on the longest day,
> With steadfast love, is caught away :
> And yet my days go on, go on."

How vivid to my mind's eye seems now the picture of that happy-faced, blooming girl, as, flushed and animated with exercise, she entered the "study-hall," receiving and returning the smiling salutations of her schoolmates with a kindness peculiarly her own. But from the moment that the first name of the roll-call was heard as the signal for the opening of school, no face was more earnest, no attitude more attentive than hers. From the reading of the scriptures and prayer, with which the daily duties begun, to the closing French recitation, her whole mind was engrossed with one thought—to improve the advantages with which she was blessed, and do her duty "as to the Lord and not to men."

As a model of an *earnest* Christian school-girl,

I have never seen her surpassed. None of her teachers or classmates would have thought of calling her mind extraordinarily brilliant; but as a conscientious student, and a seeker of truth for its own sake, all began by admiring, and ended by loving her.

With much satisfaction did Mary enter upon her last year at school, anticipating with pleasure the advanced studies which she would pursue, and the enjoyment to be taken in her music and French, yet almost sorry that her girl life was passing, and womanhood about to begin.

The future, however, so wisely hidden from view, had strange things in store for her. The first shot at Sumter, which commenced the civil war, and effected revolutions greater or less in every private as well as public circle, destroyed her father's business. The accumulation of years was locked up, as it were, in a day. Mary's knowledge of family affairs thus far had been of prosperity only, the time of *want* she had never known. Her experiences began with family comfort, and till almost eighteen years of age everything affecting her education, convenience, and pleasure had been fully provided. But the period had arrived when she was to taste adversity. In the spring of 1861, in the midst of her studies and plans, and when, like every thoughtful earnest young heart, she was anxiously wondering what the end of these strange things would be, she was surprised at being told how nearly it would affect her. She had felt and said, "We cannot give our fathers, our brothers are not old enough, let us give our little influence and our prayers on the side of the right and the true;" but she did not for a moment think the struggle would otherwise affect her till, being wholly taken into her parents' counsel, it was said to her, "Daughter, if there is war declared between the South and the North father will lose all." The event proved this prediction but too true, and a new life opened upon Mary, a difficult and toilsome one, but whose effects were ever after visible in the development of her character.

As soon as the issue became known retrenchment began; the children were taken from expensive schools, music lessons ceased, and ordinary expenditures were curtailed; servants were reduced in number, the city house was rented, and the family removed to the cottage in the country.

It would be unnecessary to say that Mary regretted leaving school in this unexpected manner; but how much of a deprivation she felt it to be, few knew at the time. She had looked forward with so much pleasure to completing her course of study under the tuition of her friend and teacher, Dr. Van Norman, that it was a great sacrifice to be called upon thus suddenly to give up those fondly cherished hopes. But the hand of Providence seemed to indicate, "thus far shalt thou go and no further;" her parents asked of her to deny herself, and unhesitatingly did she relinquish her own wishes, and cheerfully prepared for the change in her circumstances.

CHAPTER V.

IN ADVERSITY.

"If loving hearts were never lonely,
    If all they wished might always be,
Accepting what they looked for only,
    They might be glad, but not in Thee.

"We need as much the cross we bear,
    As air we breathe, as light we see;
It draws us to Thy side in prayer,
    It binds us to our strength in Thee."

WHEN settled at Scarborough the family looked inward to measure more than ever its own resources for amusement and profit; and a family school was established, with Mary for teacher. No daughter could have acted her part with more fidelity and cheerfulness. She was the life of the family: teaching her brothers and sisters, and sewing for them as well as for herself; joining in the sports of the boys, and the pastimes of the little children; she met her privations, and conformed to the altered surroundings of the family, with a cheerfulness that added new joy to every pleasure.

But these straitened circumstances were, to

Mary's mind, much alleviated by two or three extenuating ones, which she delighted to enumerate: placing first the happiness of having the family circle remain intact, while so many homes and firesides were saddened by the absence of loved ones, called to the camp-fire and the battle-field. Then they were in the country, not for a summer's short sojourn, but for a year, to watch the changing seasons with the sunshine and shadow of each, to thoroughly enjoy Nature in all her moods, and to drink in the beauty around them.

During the summer Mary endeavored to carry out a plan for study, pursuing her Latin and French with her eldest brother, and keeping up her music by constant practice with the boys and lessons on the piano to them, and continuing a judicious course of reading under the direction of her parents. To fulfill this plan, together with her duties to the family, her correspondence, and the visits of a few friends, fully occupied her time. But while thus becoming acquainted with household duties, and cultivating her intellect, she did not neglect her spiritual life, but was more than ever a "living epistle, known and read of all" that she had been with Jesus and learned of him. Truly she had learned both how to abound and to

be in need, and found godliness profitable to all
things.

A letter written during that summer time will
tell its own story :

SCARBOROUGH, *July* 11.

"DEAR COUSIN ANNIE: The 5th of this month
was grandma's seventieth birthday.   God has certainly spared her to a good long life.   O Annie, if
I can only accomplish half as much good as she
has performed in her lifetime, I was going to say
I would be satisfied; but, no, I would press on,
striving, through God's aid, to attain that high
standard of pure and undefiled religion which is
to visit the widow and the fatherless, and to keep
myself *unspotted from the world.* . . .

"Well, what do you think of the times in
which we live?   Truly, never was their like before
in the world's history, and probably never will be
again.   God grant that the right may prevail!
Don't it seem dreadful that our native land is
plunged into the midst of civil war?   O! when
will all war come to an end?   I fear not until the
Prince of Peace reigns supreme, 'from the rising
of the sun to the going down of the same.'   Have
you seen the comet out your way?   Is it not grand?

To-night is most glorious; the west is still slightly tinged with orange and yellow, the last reflection of the sun's departing rays; the moon is almost full, and shines with the brilliancy of a calcium light; the stars in their courses are shining steadily in the dark blue heavens. Truly 'the heavens declare the glory of God, and the firmament showeth his handiwork; day unto day uttereth speech, and night unto night showeth knowledge.'

"Your affectionate cousin,   "MARY."

The beautiful summer and the gorgeous autumn passed happily indeed to the home circle in the cottage, and the winter came in almost unawares. But it would be impossible for us to suppose that so different a prospect of spending the cheerless winter days and long quiet evenings awakened no regrets among the older members of the family, as they thought of the advantages of their whilom city life. It was only natural that visits of friends, the social and religious meetings of the Church, and the opportunities for mental culture from which they were now debarred, should be regretted, and the need of them sometimes keenly felt.

But in striving to make her duty a pleasure, and to bear her parents' burdens, the loving daughter

found the reward of an approving conscience, and
increased love and esteem on the part of all.
When the daily round of duties was done, the
evening was devoted to music and amusement with
the little ones; and when they were dismissed for
the night, reading, writing, and literary conversation gave occupation to the elder members of the
family.

To those friends who were privileged to share,
during this winter, in the hospitalities of the cottage, my words will not be needed to recall the
cheerful home picture of those pleasant winter
evenings; when the careworn father, forgetting his
anticipations of the morrow, and the weary mother
satisfied with seeing her loved ones happy, enjoyed
what was facetiously called "the family band," as
Mary at the piano, accompanied by her brothers,
with flute and violins, repeated the inspiriting
strains that pa so much loved, or ended the concert with "Rest for the Weary," and "Heaven is
my Home."

It was during one of these sociable evenings that
the watchful daughter discovered on her father's
brow signs of unwonted anxiety and care; in vain
she strove to cheer his heart and make him forget
his troubles; the load seemed almost too heavy for

him to bear. With a loving embrace and tender good-night kisses Mary retired to her own room, but not to sleep. No; first to cast all her care on her heavenly Father, and then, praying for wisdom to direct her, she seated herself at her desk to indite a letter, which she handed to her father in the morning, just as he left home for the city. The tears come to my eyes now as I read these loving lines, and think that she who penned them can never so counsel or console us again.

"MONDAY EVENING, *Nov.* 24.

"My beloved Father: You will look with surprise at this superscription, but my heart is full and I must write. My thoughts and affections at present are centered upon one idol; O, father, can you not guess? 'Tis upon him who is my life and light —upon you. This morning, when I read despairing looks upon your face, my heart bled for you; it is only in such cases and at such times that I find how closely every thread of my existence is tangled in an inextricable knot with yours. I have just been pleading with our common Father to have mercy upon you in this trying moment, and I feel, I *know* that he will. God is good; who can doubt his willingness to save to the uttermost? The blessed words of the Psalmist occur to me at this moment, 'God is our refuge and strength, a very present help in trouble. Therefore will not we fear though the earth be removed, and though the mountains be carried into the midst of the sea.' What a sublime faith is pictured by these words, and cannot, do not you *feel* it?

"The many vexations and cares that hourly harass your spirit are but filters through which your soul is purified for heaven.

"The great crisis through which you passed last winter nearly overcame you, yet how wonderfully God brought you through, and blessed you even more than you could ask or think; and will you allow a lesser burden to 'make you crazy,' to use your own words? No, no, dear father; when 'He giveth quietness, who then can make trouble?' and that you may possess that 'quietness' will be my constant prayer. You will come out of this trial purified like gold.

"It may be that I presume too much in thus addressing you; but I long to help you in some way, and I thought that perhaps a letter might effect my desire. You know that I do not talk much, especially when deeply affected. You may think me stoical, perhaps I appear so; but my heart is oftentimes brimfull, nearly ready to burst, and so I felt this morning. You have no doubt, I am sure, but that I love you; I glory in the possession of a father like you, and may God help me never to cause one pang of sorrow to pierce your heart. Dearest father, that God may ever be with you and give you strength equal to your day, is and will be the constant prayer of your   MARY."

The winter had now fairly set in, and its discipline upon Mary's character begun. To how many in her position would it have been a season of discontent and unhappiness, or an idle submission to its privations without striving to profit by them. But the effect of this discipline upon Mary's mind and heart became daily more visible in her increased industry, self-denial, cheerfulness, and love, and may be plainly traced in the subjoined extracts from the voluminous correspondence which she carried on with friends:

"*December* 3, 1861.

"Since we have determined to pass the winter up here, we have been so busy getting ready, and making clothes suitable for the children, that every moment has been fully occupied. You know, my

dear Louise, that the sewing for four small children is no small item in one's catalogue of duties,
and nearly all of it devolved upon me. And now
I am teaching school from nine to twelve, and after
dinner Dolph takes a music lesson; then I practice
for an hour; and the remainder of the afternoon is
devoted to sewing and taking care of the children.
. . . I wish that you could take a peep into our
parlor windows and see us as we are sitting around
the table. Pa and C. are amusing themselves,
Mason is busy, and I am writing to you. Ma and
D. are in the city.

"After all, though it is a great trial in some
respects to be cooped up here all winter, away
from our nearest and dearest friends, yet in other
respects it will be a great advantage to us. Perhaps God has some great work for me to do, and
this winter's discipline may be preparing me for it.
At all events I am very happy; my peace is made
with my Saviour, God smiles upon me and abundantly blesses me. I 'praise him for all that is past,
and trust him for all that's to come.' How true it
is that when you perform your duty with all your
might, *then* you enjoy the most peace. . . .

"I am trying to learn the hard lesson 'in whatsoever state I am, therewith to be content;' for

He hath said, 'I will never leave thee nor forsake thee.' Thrice blessed promise! Love to all my friends, especially my Sabbath-school class, and do not forget to pray for your friend   "MARY."

"*February* 1, 1862.

"It is late Saturday night, dear Louise, yet I feel that I must write a few lines to you before 1 sleep. Sometimes I have such a longing to see you that it is only by a strong effort of the will that I can control my feelings. I find my life hard sometimes, but, God be praised! I usually come out conqueror through the Beloved. . . . I am very happy in the family circle, especially in trying to do my duty. How little we know of ourselves until our faculties are exercised. I should very often fail were I not sustained by my Saviour. O how 1 love him! I will try to devote my whole energy to his service. Truly yours."

"*February* 26, 1862.

"If I only can do good, and so in some measure at least glorify my beloved Saviour, I shall not have lived in vain. I feel that

> ' Life is real! Life is earnest!
> And the grave is not its goal;
> "Dust thou art, to dust returnest,"
> Was not spoken of the soul.'

" Isn't the Psalm of Life grand ? It is so full of soul; the last verse especially touches my heart very much :

> ' Let us then be up and doing,
> With a heart for any fate ;
> Still achieving, still pursuing,
> Learn to labor and to wait.'

" I think that it is wicked.to live without an object in life, and yet how many would say, ' What can I do? my position is such that I am not able to do anything.' My answer would be to such, Life is made up of little things; one little word spoken by you may result in the conversion of many souls. Ella, sister, improve every opportunity for doing good."

" *March* 10.

" DEAR LOUISE : I have felt a strong desire to write to you, but have been unable till now. Last week mother went to the city, and was there from Tuesday until Saturday, consequently I assumed the duties of *mother*, sister, and daughter. Poor grandma, I fear, is on her death-bed. Only He who holds the issue of life and death can tell when our beloved grandma will leave this world for a brighter and better.

" Perhaps you will be surprised when I tell you

that pa has resolved to have the new house put up right away, and, God willing, we will occupy it this summer. . . .

"I trust this house will be what I have always longed for, 'a homestead,' a place where all the relatives of the family can meet once in a while and have joyous gatherings. I want it also to be a place of refuge; where, in case of trial, we shall always be welcome. God grant that none of us should ever *want* for a home! Sometimes I dream about the future, and see all our large family settled in life. I pray the Lord that there may never be a 'prodigal' in our family. But I feel with Longfellow:

> " Trust no future, howe'er pleasant;
> Let the dead past bury its dead;
> Act, act in the living present !
> Heart within, and God o'erhead."

" God bless you, my friend."

During this winter was begun that memorable institution, the " Family Journal," a source of interest and amusement to parents and children, who shared alike in the labor and pleasure attending it. A page written by Mary will find its appropriate place just here :

" *Thursday, March* 20.—Lila and I are alone in the sitting-room; anon I hear the voices of the little ones at their sports. Bless their little hearts, how I love them! Darling children! with what confidence and trust they come to me, their elder sister, in all their troubles. They often ask me strange questions, and sometimes I am sorely puzzled to answer them simply enough. Lila especially is very anxious to know the truth; she has just been asking me what is meant by ' casting out devils.' Last Sunday morning three of the children came into my room and talked about spiritual things. Lila asked why Jesus died upon the cross. I explained the best that I could, and I think that she understood it thoroughly. Pa and ma are in the city now."

About this time Mary was much interested in a volume of biography called "Leila Ada, the Jewish Convert," and finding in it a series of resolutions, which she felt were judicious and what was needed for herself, after deliberation and prayer, adopted them for her own. Too conscientious to adopt another's form of words with precipitancy, she pondered each sentence, and weighed every word, till by modifications and additions she had altered the original to suit her own circumstances; then carefully copying her first rough draft, she laid the paper in her portfolio, to be frequently perused and meditated on:

"Monday, March 23, 1862.

"I am so dissatisfied with my present mode of living, that I am resolved, God being my helper, to alter my conduct entirely, and for that purpose I resolve:

"1. That my highest aim in life shall be to glorify God in my body and spirit, which are his.

"2. That I will never be ashamed of my religion, but will always avow it, when and where it shall seem proper so to do.

"3. That I will always carefully speak the truth, never indulge in the least equivocation, but always be both verbally and substantially correct; and to this end I will carefully watch the meaning of all I utter.

"4. That I will always be ready to confess a fault and ask forgiveness for it, no matter what the character or the position of the person against whom I have offended.

"5. That I will always strive to do unto others as I would that they should do to me; that I will never do anything which, if I saw it committed by another, would cause him or her to fall in my esteem.

" 6. That, as far as in me lies, I will never do or be anything upon which I cannot expectingly and confidingly ask the blessing of God.

" 7. That when I have fixed a principle in my mind as right in the sight of God, I will never abandon it, unless convinced that it is a wrong one, or would involve me in bad consequences.

" 8. That in fulfilling a clear duty, or in the pursuit of a proper and good object I will never allow myself to be overcome by any trials or difficulties whatever.

" 9. That I will spend one hour in each day in studying the Scriptures, and communing with my heavenly Father.

" 10. That I will live to God while I do live, and strive never to engage in anything which I would shun if assured I was living the last hour of my life.

" 11. That upon all occasions I will discountenance improper levity and *conversation* in whatever company I may be.

" 12. That I will carefully guard my temper, and never show the least symptom of unpleasant emotion; not even by an altered tone of voice, or expression of countenance. That I will do this even if from physical causes I feel fretful and uneasy; no one else should suffer on this account. O my Saviour, bestow on me a double portion of grace to keep this resolution!

"13. That in my responsible situation as the eldest child, I will endeavor to set an example of purity and goodness to my brothers and sisters, that they may see daily that my life is hid with Christ in God.

"14. That I will never speak sharply or crossly to any one, but, on the contrary, I will strive to be gentle and affectionate, which will gain my desires the sooner.

"15. That I will never slander my neighbor, either by a word or expression of countenance, but always commend the good that is in him.

"16. That my whole conduct shall be governed by love, that, so doing, I may fulfill the law of Christ.

"17. That I will never waste a moment.

"18. That I will be temperate in eating and drinking.

"19. That I will strictly guard against pride in dress, and every other of its manifestations; against vanity and conceit, and indulging supposed superiority of mind.

" 20. That I will never seek my own satisfaction or pleasure at the expense of others, but, as far as possible, forget that there is a self to please.

" 21. That when confidence has been reposed in me I will never betray it.

" 22. That I will always be polite and easy in manners, urbane and gentle in company, neat and tasteful in my appearance, and in every respect show that I am a true Christian lady.

" 23. That I will honor and obey my parents m everything, love them with my whole heart, and do everything I can to promote their temporal and spiritual welfare.

" 24. That I will embrace every opportunity to improve my mind and heart, and avoid reading or conversing about anything that would demoralize my mind. *Religio et patientia et perseverantia omnia vincunt.*" " MARY F N."

" *March* 24.

" I am so glad, Ella, that spring has come; I long for my flowers. I devoutly thank my Father in heaven for having made this world so beautiful. Some people think it is such a gloomy world; perhaps it is in some respects; but God's love is so manifested in nature, that it makes the most forbidding object declare there is a God."

In a letter written April 1, after speaking to Cousin Annie of the death of a friend, Mary says:

" O what a joyful meeting we will have when we all get home to heaven! Just think of the loved ones we will meet there, friends and relatives, all to be united throughout eternity. Let us both ' run with patience the race that is set before us, looking unto Jesus the author and finisher of our faith.' For we know that we have a house not made with hands, eternal in the heavens. Has not our blessed Saviour said, ' Let not your heart be troubled; ye believe in God, believe also in me. In my Father's house are many mansions; if it were not so, I would have told you; I go to prepare a place for you. . . . I will come again and receive you unto myself, that where I am, there ye may be also.'

"I will trust in my Saviour, I will love him, and serve him to the end of my days. May God bless you, and make you, dear cousin, his faithful follower."

"*April 2.*

" DEAR ELLA: You know it is our custom to recite a verse of Scripture on Sunday mornings

6

at the breakfast table.   Mine last Sunday was as
follows: 'As ye have received Christ Jesus the
Lord, so walk in him, rooted and built up in him,
stablished in the faith as ye have been taught,
abounding therein with thanksgiving.'

" What a world of thought does this open to
us: do we follow Christ and walk in him as we
have received him ?   Alas, no !   What a thought:
'rooted and built up in Him !' our source of being,
our living head in all things !

" Christ may be compared to a noble oak, whose
branches form a protection to the beasts of the
field, and the fowls of the air lodge in them.   The
wind brings a tiny seed, and drops it at the foot of
the oak.   By and by, under the influence of the
sun and rain, tiny roots shoot down among the
roots of the great tree.   In the course of time they
grow stronger, and the earth opens and lets the
little leaves peep forth ; at first tremblingly, but
gathering more courage, they venture further, until
able to reach the trunk of the great tree.

" As days pass on the tiny seed becomes a beautiful vine, but it must have support; it looks
around, and seeing the stately oak, ventures to
cling to it.   The oak offers its protection and help,
and soon the little weak vine becomes stronger and

larger, until it is impossible to separate it from its support, the tree. Its roots and branches are so intermingled with the roots and branches of the oak, that they have become like one.

"So it should be with us; our lives and hearts should be so hid with Christ in God that they could not possibly be separated. O, Ella, the more I ponder the mysteries and wonders of earth and heaven, the more I feel my own nothingness and worthlessness. But He who notices even a sparrow when it falls to the ground will take charge of me, who am of much more value than many sparrows. 'I will trust in him; he is my portion forever.'"

"*April 2.*

"DEAR FRIEND ADDIE: We have been spending the winter here in the country, and I can assure you it is very different from living in the city. My father rented our house in the city for economy. I suppose nearly every one has been obliged to retrench in his expenses this winter; it seems hard, don't it? But not our will, but thine, O Lord, be done.

"Yet we have spent a very happy winter; we have really experienced what 'evenings at home' are, for being obliged to stay in-doors, we have spent our evenings very pleasantly with music, reading, and sewing. Not being able to attend school, we organized a home school, with myself for the teacher of four children, the babies being too young to attend; and I pursued my own studies with C. We have tried to improve, and I think that some of us have made considerable progress.

" On the whole, I think we have passed a profitable winter. I am glad that spring has come; I long to cultivate my flowers. I take great pleasure in watching their development. In the summer I intend to have a nice flower-garden.   .

" This winter I have had nearly the entire charge of the four children, and I can assure you it is no small task. But I love to have them come to me, and with their little earnest faces ask me questions with the confidence so beautiful to see between brothers and sisters. It is a great responsibility to lead their little minds heavenward, and instruct them in the way of holiness. May the Lord give me grace and patience sufficient for my station and duty."

"*April* 16.

" 'Tis a lovely day, dear Louise; how you would enjoy looking at the river were you here; the waters are so calm and quiet that the mountains are plainly and beautifully reflected.

" The various sounds iudicative of life are distinctly audible. The hum of distant voices, the deep baying of dogs, the twitter of birds, and the low of cattle, all proclaim that ' life is real.' The most precious thought to me is that God, the immortal, the invisible, ' sitteth on the throne and ruleth all things.'

" Sometimes I long for the day when my freed soul will wing its way to the New Jerusalem. At times my soul is bowed to the dust, and I grow weary of earth; but a voice like that of the Son of God whispers, '.Be of good cheer, I have overcome the world.' I have a work to do here on earth, and I must

> ' Be up and doing,
> With a heart for any fate,'

and in due season I shall be at rest ' if my faith fail not.'

" May the Lord be with you in whatever you do, is the prayer of your friend."

" *May* 15.

" I bless and praise God with you, dear Ella, for his abundant mercy and long-suffering. What a forbearing Father we have! how he loves us, and with what compassion he regards our weaknesses! I am overwhelmed when I think on these things. I think I can say that I love my God 'with all my heart, and soul, and mind, and strength;' but I have not yet arrived at that pure, unselfish condition where I can 'love my neighbor as myself.' The process will be gradual, but I trust sure; and by my Saviour's help I may ere long become pure and unselfish. I am naturally very willful, selfish, and passionate; when these three giants are overcome, I may then hope to set an example of goodness to others."

"*May* 17.

"MY DEAR COUSIN: It was with deep pleasure and gratitude that I perused your letter. I felt especially thankful that you had proved yourself a ministering angel at the sickbed of a dying saint. God will bless and reward you, dear cousin, for your kindness. Have you not often realized that 'it is more blessed to give than to receive?' The longer I live, the more I am convinced that our Saviour never spoke one idle word; he spoke nothing but truth.

"Is not the country enchanting in spring? If earth is so wondrously beautiful, what must heaven be, to which earth is but as 'dust in the balance!'

It has been so long since I have passed a spring in the country, or had an opportunity to watch the development of nature, that I am perfectly enrap- tured with the sights that meet me on every hand. Is it not beautiful to see the fruit trees all laden with fragrant blossoms?

"Well, I hope we progress as much in wisdom as we do in years. How bitterly I regret, now that I am deprived of my school privileges, that I did not improve my time more diligently. Do make the most of your school days, for a period will sometime come when you will say, 'O, days of my youth, return, return!'"

"*May* 30.

"O how my soul has exulted in beholding the bursting beauty of the country this season! I never before passed a spring in the country when I could appreciate its surpassing loveliness. It has been remarked that this spring the country has bloomed with more than ordinary beauty. Every little while I run to the window and exclaim, how lovely! and my soul experiences the most exquisite pleasure while drinking its fill from God's goblet of beauty and goodness. I say again, dear Ella, if earth is so perfectly beautiful, what must heaven be! God grant we may both reach that blissful shore, and perhaps, Ella, we may wander hand in hand along the banks of the River of Life, and converse about and compare the beauty of this world with that far brighter one.

"Sometimes I grow so weary of earth that I can hardly wait until my Lord sees fit to take me home. This verse has arrested my attention very closely: 'Whom having not seen, ye love; in whom, though now ye see him not, yet believing, ye rejoice with joy unspeakable and full of glory.' What truth and depth there is to that passage, 'whom having not seen, ye love.'

'I love Thee, I love Thee, and that Thou dost know,
But how much I love Thee I never can show.'"

In writing of the death of a friend Mary says:

"*June 9.*

"Our friends are taken away on every side, one by one, and who will be next? Perhaps you, perhaps I. But I hope that for us to die will be gain. 'O death, where is thy sting? O grave, where is thy victory?' 'I know that my Redeemer liveth, and that he shall stand at the latter day upon the earth; and though after my skin worms destroy this body, yet in my flesh shall I see God.' 'The

Spirit and the bride say, Come. And let him that heareth say, Come. And let him that is athirst come. And whosoever will, let him take the water of life freely.' 'He that testifieth these things saith, Surely I come quickly: Amen. Even so, come, Lord Jesus.' O how I long to go home and be at rest! to lay my weary, aching head upon my Saviour's bosom. But I must finish the work that Thou gavest me to do, and then, O the inexpressible joy of always being with Him whom my soul loves! Does not earth seem tame when compared with heaven? But hush! my beating heart; thou must suffer like unto thy Saviour, and when thy strength is perfect through suffering thou shalt find rest."

"*July* 24.

"DEAR ANNIE: Do you build castles in the air much? That is one of my favorite amusements: my hands move mechanically at my work, but my imagination takes wings and tries to peer into the dim regions of futurity, but in vain; the great gates of 'To Come' are closed and sealed as with adamant. I often wish that I could know what will be my future life, but it is well that God alone possesses that knowledge. I am content to live each day as if it were my last; has not

He said, 'Sufficient unto the day is the evil thereof?'

"Doesn't this *war* seem to you like some terribly appalling panorama? Can you realize it? I can hardly believe that our own native land, the land we love the most, 'the land of the free and the home of the brave,' is desolated by war, rebellion, and treason. They tell me that there have been fearful battles, and that thousands of hearth-stones are desolate. 'Mothers, weeping for their children, will not be comforted because they are not.'

"It must be some terrible dream. But no! 'tis all too true: the Lord has covered his face, his vengeance is poured out upon us. Haven't we suffered enough?

"O, our Father, have mercy upon us.

"O Lord, have mercy upon us.

"Listen! do you hear that still, small voice, so sweet and melodious, saying, 'God is our refuge and strength, a very present help in trouble. Therefore will we not fear, though the earth be removed, and though the mountains be carried into the midst of the sea; though the waves thereof roar and be troubled, though the mountains shake with the swelling thereof."

"July 25.

"I can never do enough for my blessed Saviour; but if, after doing what I can, my Lord shall say, 'Well done, good and faithful servant,' my cup of bliss will be full."

We find this entry in the "Family Journal:"

"July 30, (1862 :) This afternoon has witnessed one of the most frightful and terrific storms of the season. The north and west were shrouded with angry black clouds; distant mountains were hidden in the gloom. The clear blue waters of the Hudson reflected the angry visage of the heavens, and all nature betokened a display of the Omnipotent in all his majesty and terror. Ere long the rain fell in torrents, accompanied with occasional booms of thunder, and quick vivid flashes of lightning. The rain increased with such violence that the roads became ponds, and our cucumber bed appeared like a lakelet dotted with green islands. Suddenly, crack, smash, bang! Hailstones varying in size from a pea to a bantam's egg began to fly in all directions. Woe betide any poor craven out of shelter. This peppering of hail lasted upward of thirty minutes. Suddenly the black ominous clouds broke away, and the sun poured forth his

beams on a crest-fallen earth. Windows smashed,
grass and flowers beaten flat, corn-leaves torn to
ribbons, newly-worked roads rendered almost im-
passable with ruts, stones, and mud.

"Grandma says that in forty years she has not
seen such a violent hailstorm; and certainly the
younger members of the family beheld with awe
and wonder the vengeance nature poured forth
upon the earth, this being their first experience
of the kind."

"*August* 21.

"DEAR ADDIE : I aspire to be a thoroughly good
woman, devoted heart and soul to my God, my
family, and my country. And to this end I strive
to build up a character, with divine help, which
will in the end make me such a one."

"*August* 25.

"The ninth of August, dear Louise, was my
birthday, and I have reached the advanced age
of nineteen. Well, I do feel very old, far older
in years than in judgment; I suppose that I will
always be a child in some respects. Pa gave me
a beautiful locket containing his own and ma's
likeness. I often look at it and kiss the dear faces
imprinted thereon. God bless my father and
mother, and make me worthy of such parents.

"When you see the votaries of fashion and worldly pleasure living for nothing but this world, do you not feel a sincere pity for them, and thank God that you have been called to follow the highest calling to which a human being can attain—a child of God—an heir of heaven?

"I will give you my favorite motto; its spirit has carried me through many a difficult task: '*Perseverantia et patientia omnia vincunt.*'"

As the Christian is known equally by what he *fears* as by what he hopes, it may be expedient to copy *verbatim* from Mary's journal a leaf or two written at this time:

"*Sept.* 28.—I feel constrained to pen a few words to-day; perhaps it may relieve my heavy heart. Life has been very pleasant, and I trust profitable, during the last two years. Responsibilities more weighty than ever before have fallen to my lot; but as my day, so has my strength been. My father's circumstances being greatly reduced, we were necessarily deprived of many luxuries; but I care little for that. I assumed almost the entire charge of the younger children, but that is as nothing compared with my heart-struggles. To-day I could cover my head with

dust and ashes, crying 'Unclean, unclean.' My
defects stare me in the face, so glaringly and
tauntingly that I feel crushed to the very earth. I
wonder that my parents and friends will own me,
being nothing but a disgrace to them; but worse
than all, I have crucified my Saviour afresh.
Proudly confident of my own strength, I have
rushed madly into forbidden paths, and God by
mortifying means has acquainted me with my
error.

"I feel humbled; my spirit is broken. Discouraged and cast down, I find little to comfort
me but my earnest intention and desire to commence anew. God helping me I'll try, but I am
so fearful of again falling into error. But this
trial will prove beneficial in its results; my wicked
pride needs this discipline to subdue it entirely to
the will of my heavenly Father.

"I look forward to the coming winter with
pleasure and interest, it being my earnest intention to devote more time to the service of the
Lord. I think I can conscientiously declare that
if I fail on all other points, yet patience has begun
her perfect work in me. I am going now to bow
myself in prayer that the Lord will aid me to do
better."

"DEAR ANNIE: This morning early four little children, with the assistance of their sister, were busily engaged donning their habiliments for the morning, when an exclamation from grandma drew our attention to the western sky. Dipping in the river appeared one end of that grand old ' bow of promise,' and sweeping northward, disappeared in the radiant heavens. Surely fainting hearts might take courage from such a glorious vision—proclaiming God is love. My own heart imbibes the freshness of this lovely day, and is strengthened for this day's duties, conflicts, and pleasures.

"Go·on, Annie, study all that you can, and you will never repent it; but don't forget to improve the heart even more than the mind, 'for out of *it* are the issues of life.' Solemn and wonderful is our mission on earth.

> ' A charge to keep I have,
>   A God to glorify;
> A never-dying soul to save,
>   And fit it for the sky.'

"Annie, are you a Christian? You never mention the subject in your letters. Do tell me, and O how my heart will rejoice should you answer in the affirmative."

In the "Family Journal," October 19 : "The holy calm of the Sabbath pervades the land. The morning light dawned upon the household, gently rousing it from slumber, and demanding the praise due the Creator. Cheerfully and willingly our hearts and voices joined in adoration to the Father of mercies, and receiving a Sabbath morning bless-ing, we felt determined to spend the day faith-fully in the service of the Lord."

Thus have we revived the memories of our loved one through the vicissitudes and unusual burdens of the year and a half, and we have seen how nobly she bore her part. And though Mary, as well as her parents, believed that their heavenly Father, "too wise to err, too good to be unkind," was preparing them by this severe disci-pline for some future usefulness, how little did any suspect what the trial of their faith would be.

> "God keeps a niche
> In heaven to hold our idols; and albeit
> He brake them to our faces, and denied
> That our close kisses should impair their white—
> I know we shall behold them raised, complete,
> The dust swept from their beauty—glorified."

CHAPTER VI.

SUNNY MEMORIES.

"I doubt if she said to you much that could act
As a thought or suggestion; she did not attract
In the sense of the brilliant or wise: I infer
'Twas her thinking of others made you think of her."

BY the autumn of this year business in the metropolis had so much recovered from the shock it experienced at the beginning of the war, and the father's new enterprises had been so successful, that the family returned to the city early in November. The boys resumed their studies at school, and Mary was in a measure relieved from some of the care and responsibility which had been hers so long. She still instructed her sisters, and labored to improve her own mind and heart.

Her parents, sympathizing in the regret at discontinuing her studies so unexpectedly, determined to give her every advantage in their power during this winter. Accordingly much pains were bestowed on her music and French, and arrangements made for private lessons in a more advanced

7

course of English studies under her pastor and friend, Dr. True. Mary took much delight in the discussions arising from "Upham" and "Cousin," and in our walks to the parsonage would frequently say, "Now, Louise, I want to have the doctor explain this or that," mentioning an objection or opinion developed in her mind by the lesson of the previous day; showing that she did not consider her work done when the recitation was finished and the text-book closed, but made the subject of her studies frequent themes for meditation. Dr. T., writing of this interesting period, says:

"While pastor of the Thirtieth-street Methodist Episcopal Church in New York I formed a class in mental philosophy at the request of friends, to meet at the parsonage four or five mornings in the week. The class consisted of Mary N., Louise C., and Emily T., and met for the first time December 9, 1862. We began with Upham's Mental Science, and afterward took up and read Cousin's Critique of Locke. My recollections of this class are among the most pleasant reminiscences of my life as a teacher. Mary surprised me by the thoroughness of her mastery of every lesson, and the clearness of her recitations. I had before thought of her only as a beautiful girl of amiable disposition and bright understanding in common things; but I had no expectation that she would penetrate very deeply into the abstrusities of mental science. On this account I selected the plainest and most attractive treatise on the subject which is used in our best seminaries; but when we had left the illustrated pages of Upham, and entered the higher regions of metaphysics with the acute and pervasive Cousin, I found Mary as capable of penetrating his meaning, comprehending his arguments, and appreciating and feeling his subtle eloquence, as the best student in college. She studied not only with diligence but with enthusiasm the whole of that masterly criticism by which the great eclectic has forever overthrown the dominion of Locke's sensationalism, and placed it in a just and honorable subordination to a true idealism.

"At that time Mary was in the full bloom of womanhood, without any symptoms of decline, except that she had a cough which we all hoped was but a transient cold. I am persuaded that her metaphysical studies gave a healthy development to her mind, raised her ideas of God and the universe, gave her a deeper consciousness of freedom and virtue, and inspired her with brighter hopes of immortality. During her last illness I

am grateful to know she recurred often to the
happy hours we had spent in discussion of these
grand topics, and cheered her languid hours
with such speculations as she had been taught
to indulge.

"Adieu, my loved pupil; the bright reason that
shone so cloudlessly in you, if not the divine
Logos himself in you was certainly his brightest image, and being a creature perfect after its
kind, was the best proof of the existence of that
all-perfect intelligence which alone could be its
Creator; and its far revealings beyond the range
of the senses was in you proof of its immortality,
being so distinct from the material organism as not
to share its doom of dissolution, but to be all the
more alive and active by the falling off of those
fleshly organs on whose impressions, by their contact with the external world, it was at first depend-
ent, as the occasions of the unfolding of its almost
divine intuitions."

Mary also resumed her labors in the Sabbath-
school by taking a class of ten little girls, who soon
loved her dearly. She took much pleasure also in
attending the religious meetings during the week;
and on one occasion, walking home together, she
said, "Louise, I think there is more real com-

fort and happiness in going to a prayer-meeting, such as we have enjoyed to-night, than any votary of pleasure can experience by attendance at ball or opera. How thankful we ought to be that we have been educated by Christian parents."

A letter to her grandmother, written a fortnight after they came to the city, presents a charming picture of innocent enjoyment:

"NEW YORK, *November* 15, 1862.

"MY DEAR GRANDMA: Two weeks to-day have we been residents of this great metropolis. Varied indeed is our life compared with the lovely quiet of our peaceful country home. All was so beautiful there, where God and nature reigned supreme; but here, how shall I describe it? Nearly everything and everybody appears so superficial; no heart, nothing but the accomplishment of their own selfish ends. We like our house very well. Some things might be more agreeable, but

'Every pleasure hath its pain,
And every sweet a snare.'

"The children feel the confinement very much, though I take them out nearly every day. On pleasant afternoons a young lady may be seen walking the streets, attended by four frisking specimens of humanity, said young lady having a wonderfully resigned expression resting on her countenance. Picture to your imagination what it must be to cross a muddy avenue with the four; but I really enjoy going out with them.

"Monday night a very large missionary meeting was held at Bedford-street. Pa, C., D., and I went. Quite a number of distinguished ministers spoke, among them Bishops Janes and Simpson. O, grandma, when I gazed upon those noble men growing old in the service of their Master, I felt great reverence for them. Bishop Janes, with his soft, gentle accents, and quiet, persuasive manner, calmed us; but when Bishop Simpson reared his great form aloft and fairly thundered, every passion and emotion of our natures was on fire. Never had I seen him before, and great as was my reverence, its depth is tenfold greater since I have seen and heard him. Bishop Baker was present also. Dr. T. walked home with us, and we all felt better for having been in the ennobling presence of great men.

"The Monday after we came to the city pa came home early with the intelligence that Claude B. was dead. After a severe illness of seventeen days she fell asleep in Jesus. Perhaps there never was a sweeter death than hers. When she found that life was very short she meekly kissed the rod, and said, 'Thy will be done!' Beautifully did she exhibit that

> 'Jesus can make a dying bed
> Feel soft as downy pillows are.'

"No murmur or complaint escaped her lips. Her pastor was with her a great deal, and she would tell him to talk to her of heavenly things. She said, 'Tell all my friends that nothing is worth living for but the preparation for this dying hour.' As she was dying she folded her hands on her breast and closed her eyes. Her mother noticed her lips moving, and bending over her said, 'What is it Claude?' She shook her head, as if to say she could not answer, but her mother caught the word 'faith.'

"She lay in an open coffin, clad in purest white, with white flowers scattered about her person. On her breast lay a beautiful crown of flowers, and just below it a cross, beautifully expressive that those who bear the cross shall wear the crown. Death was most lovely in her case, and I could not but mentally exclaim, 'Let me die the death of the righteous.'"

The death of this lovely young Christian made a great impression on Mary, and contributed in no small degree to dispel from her mind all aversion to conversation in reference to her own feelings in prospect of dying. It was the first time she had ever looked upon death, and it is remarkable that her own passing away and funeral service should so much resemble Claude's.

Another. letter to the young friend whom she had so often urged to be decided for the Saviour's cause, seems to tell us that her "labor had not been in vain:"

"*December* 27.

"MY DEAR ADDIE: Your father was almost ready to go when you last wrote to me, and now he is singing with the angels in heaven.* Your affliction and sorrow cannot be greater at losing him than it was at seeing him suffer so intensely, and feeling that every moment might leave you fatherless. But, Addie, I know that you are a Christian, and your trust is firmly placed on Him 'who doeth all things well.' And you cannot but rejoice in prospect of your dear father's eternal

---

* At the time this was written it was thought that the person referred to was deceased, but in fact he recovered and is still living.

happiness. Think of him as a glorified being, bearing the impress of God's elect, treading the golden streets of the New Jerusalem in company with Abraham, Isaac, and Jacob, walking on the banks of the River of Life, and saying, as did Christian of old, 'I heartily thank my God and King for bringing me to this place.' And, dear Addie, while thinking this of him, make a firm resolve, God helping you, to meet him there.

"Think what a responsibility rests upon you. Deprived of a father's care and love, your brothers and sisters naturally look to your mother, but she is growing old, and will lean heavily on you; and may God in his mercy strengthen you for your position and its duties. And be assured he will do it; you can do all things through Christ strengthening you.

"Your friend,   "MARY."

The following, to Mary's cousin Annie, is the last of this winter's correspondence which we are privileged to read:

"NEW YORK, *February* 28.

"DEAREST COUSIN: Our parlor at present presents a quiet, cheerful home scene. Pa, C., D., and myself surround the center table. The three former are studying their Sunday-school lessons, while I am writing to you. Our venerable grandma sits near the register enjoying thoughts of the past, and dwelling on the future. Is there any place like home? *O domum dulce, dulce domum!* We mingle with the world, travel, visit, and wander from our loved ones, but in our most secret heart *home* is engraven, like *Calais* on Queen Mary's.

"I read a most beautiful sentiment the other day, which I will insert here for your reflection. Some one, speaking of the wonderful love of our Father in heaven, says: 'Love is the king of words, carved on Jehovah's heart.' Is it not beautiful?

"This winter has passed swiftly and delightfully with me. Temporally, God has abundantly blessed us; and spiritually, my heart has been turned toward my risen Saviour; and if I have not advanced as much toward the entire subjection of self to the will of God, I have this consciousness, that I *desire* not to be worldly. O how often have I tried to leave self out of the question; but, Annie, when we think that self is conquered, we find it creeping from underneath some beautiful flower. This is such a sweet comfort to me—that my Saviour was 'tempted in all points as we are, yet without sin;' and with every temptation there is provided 'a way of escape.'

"It seems as if I love you, dear Annie, a great deal more since assurance has been given me that you are numbered among the people of God. May he ever keep you faithful, is the prayer of

"MARY."

Here ends the record of that happy, peaceful winter. And all Mary's friends in the city cannot but rejoice in remembering how it was granted to them to enjoy her society during this little season of her perfect health.

Perhaps it is more true in a large family than in others, that "something is happening most years." This six months' sojourn in New York had not been without incident. The little children had all been very ill with the measles, and the thought that her eldest brother would leave home in the fall had given at times a shade of sadness to the family group; but through all, Mary had enjoyed such rest as those only enter into who walk in the strait and narrow path of duty.

Some of her friends had noticed in Mary, during

the winter, an inclination to cough, and were not surprised, as spring came on, to hear that she had left home for a visit to her uncle at Lima. This change of air, it was fondly hoped, would be beneficial to her, and so for a season it seemed.

Mary enjoyed her visit exceedingly; no less the journey and sight-seeing than the more intimate acquaintance with her relatives, whom she had not seen since leaving school. During her stay at Lima a little incident occurred which her cousin loves to recall. They had been spending the evening out, and returning home about nine o'clock had seated themselves upon the porch to enjoy the moonlight.

From speaking of the pleasure of the evening and the beauty of the night, they strayed on in their talk to more serious subjects, when Mary said, "Annie, I have often wondered who of our large family would be the first to go; I have always felt as if I would." Then they talked about when they would rather die, before or after their parents, and each thought she could better bear the pain of parting than father or mother could; and Mary said she hoped to live; "but, Annie, let us remember this conversation, and whichever is taken first let the other be comforted by it."

On Mary's return from Lima the family removed to Ashridge to spend the summer, those golden, happy days, the last which they were to spend together as an unbroken circle.

The letters which we here append mark how the days passed till the first link in the family chain was broken, and C. left for college; his leave-taking to be followed by another only more regretted, that of Mary herself; but we must not anticipate.

"ASHRIDGE, *May* 6, 1863.

"DEAR ANNIE: Are you a teacher in the Sunday-school? I felt very sorry to part with my little girls when we left New York. I had ten as lovely little scholars as you could well find. They used to watch so eagerly for me, and when I appeared, their eager, expectant faces would brighten so quickly that I could catch them all to my heart and keep them there. Darling children! I wonder whether they will have any teacher who will love them better than I did. But O, I was not as faithful as I ought to have been. I allowed too many opportunities to pass which I might have improved. But I will strive to have no regrets in the future if God permits me to live and work. MARY."

"*May* 13.

"MY DEAR LOUISE : How welcome your letter was to me. I had felt real lonesome, because you know the change was considerable—from the city, where I could see some of my friends every day, to here, where hardly any company is seen, except the workmen, the butcher, and the grocer. Those rainy days it was dreary enough, but what am I saying? I fear it will sound like discontent; but don't take it so, for I am happy as far as external circumstances are concerned; But O, Louise, I am so troubled about myself. I scarcely know what is the matter, my heart is dull, dead, cold; I fear religion is a mere name with me. I long so earnestly to do right, and mechanically try to perform my allotted duties; but what does that amount to if the Holy Spirit does not abide in me. Tell me what to do. I pray and read my Bible, and try to throw some life into my devotions. Merciful God,

'Take my poor heart, and let it be
Forever closed to all but Thee ;
Seal Thou my breast, and let me wear
The pledge of love forever there.'

But I wont talk any more about myself, it's not worth while.

"The country looks very charming since the

rain. When we first came up the trees were just budding, and looked very bare; but now they are covered with a tender green, and some of the fruit trees are in full blossom.

"But the river! how can I describe it, so solemn, and stable, and grand; its ceaseless waves the same yesterday, to-day, and till the end of the world. And our Father made them all! How can I be so distrustful, when I see his name, *Love*, written on the tiniest leaflet as well as on the firmament.

"You say you enjoyed our winter's study very much; so did I. Last winter was as pleasant a one as I ever spent, and I know that I am better and stronger than I was six months ago.

"God be with you my dear friend."

The following, written shortly after her twentieth birthday, shows the determination with which she entered on this year, which was to be such an eventful one to her:

"August 20.

"'Tis the eve of the holy Sabbath, and sweet peaceful thoughts have stirred my soul, and with them came thoughts of you, my dear cousin.

"This afternoon was the celebration of the Lord's Supper, and though we did not attend, on account

of the extraordinary and excessive heat, still my
thoughts have been with Him who, eighteen hundred years ago, said, 'Take, eat; this is my body
which is *broken for you:* this do in remembrance
of *me.*' Likewise, 'Drink ye all of this; this is my
blood which is shed for you.'

"O, Annie, did he suffer all that for you, for me?
O boundless love! who but the blessed Saviour
would have undergone such agony for sinful humanity! Annie, dear, thanks be unto God, that
both you and I have believed that his most precious
blood had power to 'cleanse us from all unrighteousness,' and we know that the 'white stone' is
given unto us bearing the impress of pardon.

"I feel so happy this afternoon. I never experience any of that ecstacy of which I've heard some
speak; but my happiness is so calm and peaceful.
I seem to understand what the Saviour meant when
he said, 'My peace I give unto you.' Yet I do
not always enjoy this; my spirit is too easily ruffled
with the vexations of life. O that my soul possessed itself in patience! Never will I be satisfied
until my heart is thoroughly imbued with the
spirit of my Saviour, so that though cares and dis-
appointments may encompass me, my strength may
never fail, for 'all my springs' will be in him.

"Read the twenty-fifth psalm, and see if it does not express the desire of your heart: 'Lead me in thy truth, and teach me, for thou art the God of my salvation; on thee do I wait all the day.' Annie, let us pray fervently for each other.

"Trusting in my all-sufficient Father, I have entered this year determined to be a Christian woman in every sense of the word; a faithful, dutiful daughter, a devoted, cheerful sister, and a true friend; in short to be a sunbeam. Do you think that such a victory awaits me? I am sure of it, if I go forth clad in the whole armor of God.

"Lovingly,   "MARY."

"*August* 27.

"You must have had a delightful trip this summer, dear Ella. I imagine how you enjoyed it. What glorious beauties nature possesses! And could you not say with the poet, 'These are thy glorious works, Parent of good?'

"From our front piazza we enjoy the most varied, perfect, and splendid view that mortal ever saw. We ought to grow to be beautiful Christians in the midst of so much that is pure and lovely. We come in contact with very little evil. I know for myself that no evil worth mentioning assails
8

me, except from my own heart. I suffer very little
temptation. And I do believe and hope that this
purity is being developed in me; I enjoy sweet
peace from God my Father."

And now the happy summer was almost gone,
and with it, one bright day, departed Mary's
companion and most intimate friend, her eldest
brother.

Perhaps in nothing is the difference between the
young and those advanced in life so noticeable,
as in the varied anticipations they enjoy and the
hopes they cherish. To a family of young people,
brought up together, and forming a little world in
themselves, all change in the home circle seems far
distant—all vacant chairs as if in a few days to be
again occupied; or, if they seriously contemplate
separations, they are to be tearless partings, and
frequent happy returnings; while those older, who
know so well,

> 'There is no union here of hearts
> Which finds not here an end,'

are more apt to look with stoicism or indifference
on the grief of youth when it discovers how bitter
is the pang of parting, and that time as well as
death works changes in all.

No indifference did these parents affect when they sent forth their eldest son, but with him sent as much of a happy home as he could carry—a father's counsel, a mother's prayers; and the deep love of all found vent in many tender lines to the quiet student far away. From among these letters we gather passages of two of Mary's

"August 27, 1863.

" I pray God every day that grace may be given me to perform the sacred duty and trust of a sister faithfully. It is no task for me to labor for my precious brothers.

" The air this morning is delightful, infusing new life into our bodies. You have seen the landscape look just as it does now, the waters are so blue and calm. As I have read, ' the great heart of the water throbbed gently as the bosom of a sleeping child.' The ships look like so many white-winged messengers of peace floating calmly on the waters of truth. Blue, you know, means truth."

" Sabbath, August 30.

"I wonder, dear brother, how you are and what your experience is this holy Sabbath morning ! this, the first Sabbath you have ever spent away alone from the home of your love, the Christian home of your childhood. Can you realize the infinite advantage you have over your companions? Surely never were children more blessed than we have been, surrounded from our birth by holy influences, and our first lispings directed to pronounce the holy name of our God. We cannot realize what the world calls sin; our main trouble is from fightings within.

"This morning has passed so pleasantly with me. I read a while with the children, and then retired to my *sanctum sanctorum*, there to commune with my Father in heaven.

"Last night Cousin Mina asked me whether I enjoyed that 'peace which passeth all understanding.' I told her that sometimes I was puzzled to know. Uniformly I felt very happy, but I feared it too often arose from indifference. But I think I am a Christian from this fact, that my life, I believe, is governed by Gospel principles, though too often I fail in executing them.

"This morning I have been questioning my heart, and this is the result: Too much confidence is placed in self, and till that idol is destroyed, peace cannot abide. While probably you were worshiping in church, I was pleading with the

Lord for more light, more humility, and more
love. Then I prayed that our blessed Saviour's
presence might rest upon you, and that you might
experience the blessedness of a Father's forgiveness.
C., have your sister's prayers been answered?

"Mina left me a sweet little book to read
while she was gone to church, called 'None Like
Christ.' It is beautifully written, and commences
by saying that the law of contrast is always studied
by the poet, painter, or logician, and the author
intends to pursue the same plan with the character
of Christ, putting it in contrast with things temporal.
The author depicts glaringly the depravity of humanity in substituting everything inferior to the
Saviour for the Saviour himself. 'It may be your
daily calling, or some pleasure of memory, or some
object of taste: music, sculpture, painting, litera-
ture, science, whatever the master-passion of your
soul, the supreme, all-engrossing object of your
life—it is your Christ, your Saviour, your beloved,
your all; and with this your only portion and
preparation, you are in a little while to confront
the bar of God! Where your treasure is there
will your heart be also.'

"I have quoted thus largely because we are
both guilty, I am confident. Examine closely, and

discover what that idol may be, and pluck it out with God's help.

"The author then dwells beautifully upon the glory of Christ: 'Can you with the exulting evangelist exclaim, "We have seen his glory, the glory of the only-begotten of the Father, full of grace and truth." "We all, with open face beholding as in a glass the glory of the Lord, are changed into the same image, from glory to glory, even as by the Spirit of the Lord."' C., think of that: 'We are all changed into the same image!' 'I shall be satisfied when I awake in thy likeness.'

" I wish you had this little book; it is full of the loveliness of our Redeemer. I feel quite happy now; my heart drinks in a portion of the peace which 'He giveth his beloved.'

" Dear Charlie, may this be a happy and a profitable day to you, and may the mantle of peace and mercy be yours is a sister's prayer. Remember, you must bear your cross at all times, and do all the good that lies in your power. Work while it is day, for the night cometh when no man can work. God Almighty bless you, dear brother."

In the following Mary speaks of her feelings in regard to the separation from her brother :

" September 4.

"DEAR LOUISE: I must begin with the subject nearest my heart, indeed all our hearts—the first link broken in our family circle by brother Charlie's absence. I little knew how dear he had become till separated from him.

" I don't pretend to play the piano, music seems so dull without the sweeter tones of his flute mingling with my deeper accompaniment.

" You know what a trial it must be to have him absent. We have been together for eighteen years; seldom disagreed, always rejoicing in each other's hopes, and sorrowing in each other's griefs; but I am thankful that his lot is cast at M——.

"I had almost forgotten to tell you that I've been troubled with a severe cough for nearly six weeks. I took cold in the early part of August, and it settled immediately into a hacking cough, very different from the one I had last winter. I have grown quite thin and pale for me. I am picking up some now, and my cough, I hope, is getting better.

"I am very well spiritually, better than in the early summer, still I cannot be satisfied until 'I awake in His likeness.' Pray for me that my faith may be stronger. God bless and keep you, my dear."

The next letter, written a little later in Septem ber, is to the mother of Mary's former pastor, an "elect lady," who honored Mary with a friendship at once happy and useful:

"*September* 13, 1863.

"VERY DEAR AND RESPECTED FRIEND: You can little imagine the joy that possessed me upon the receipt of a letter from you.

"The good seed contained therein has sunk deep in my heart, which I earnestly and constantly beseech the great *Tiller* to transform into good ground, and may the Lord grant that abundant fruit may be produced to the honor and glory of his name. For some time I have wished to write to you, but negligence and company have prevented. So to-day I determined should be partly passed in writing to you.

"The practice of writing ordinary letters on Sunday I think is very wrong; but it seems just- ifiable to write on religious themes to a holy woman like yourself, whose life is hid with Christ in God, and from whom I can receive light in regard to the way in which I but feebly grope. I have written

very few letters on Sunday, and they were purely
religious. Please tell me your views on this
subject. My fear is, that I may be doing on the
Lord's day that which should be done at another
time.

"'The Lord gave and the Lord taketh away;
blessed be the name of the Lord.' Such, I know, is
the language of your heart to-day. God has seen
fit to bereave you of another child, grief will bear
you down for a while, but this rainbow cloud will
break in a shower of mercies on your head. I
know, dear Mrs. F., that I cannot sympathize with
you as I would. God has never afflicted me with
the loss of any near and dear one, but what sympathy I possess is with you.

"Poor little children! how they will miss a tender mother's care. May God sustain you all, and
sanctify this affliction to your good. If not too
painful for you, will you please tell me more particularly about your daughter. We did not know
her as well nor see her as often as the others.

"Our home is very bright and peaceful now,
though we miss our dear C. very much, but feel
reconciled to the separation, knowing it is for his
good. I ought to grow very good with two such
bright examples before me as my parents.

" This summer my mind has been very peaceful; I am conscientiously striving to live uprightly. The heights and depths of the love of God I have not yet attained, but hope and pray that I may experience them ere long.

"Can you not come and visit us in our quiet home ? We will do all we can to make you happy. Please remember me kindly to all, and accept my sincere love for yourself; and I pray that you 'may be able to comprehend with all saints what is the breadth, and length, and depth, and height, and to know the love of Christ' that you may be filled with all the fullness of God.

"Lovingly and respectfully yours."

In a former letter Mary speaks of a hacking cough, which she found it so difficult to remove by ordinary remedies, but which was not thought serious. As the autumn, however, advanced, and no improvement in her symptoms was visible, it was decided by the physician's advice to try a change of air, in hope of a complete recovery. As her uncle and family were on the eve of departure for New Orleans, it was arranged that Mary should accompany them, trusting that the sea voyage and a short sojourn in a milder climate would restore her to perfect health. Mary announces this plan to her cousin by letter :

"ASHRIDGE, *November* 5.

"DEAR COUSIN : Please God, a week from Satday I shall be on the great ocean bound for New Orleans. This ugly cough will kill me if not checked ; for three months it has racked my frame until I have grown quite thin and pale ; all medicine seems in vain ; indeed the doctor says it will be of little avail, and consequently ordered me to sea.

The difficulty is in my throat, a most insatiable irritation which will become pulmonary if neglected. Uncle T. and his family expect to sail for New Orleans Saturday after next, and I am to accompany them.

"I anticipate pleasure from the trip, of course, though it will be hard to leave home just as my brother comes home for vacation. However, a good God will direct all for the best. Into thy hands we commit our all, for our trust is in thee O Lord, our strength and our Redeemer.

"Annie, if I leave home, I go with the full determination to do all in my power for the service of my Master. If a word in season, a pure example, a heart full of love and zeal for God will accomplish anything, I pray and believe they will not be wanting. Pray fervently for me that an Almighty Hand may ever lead me."

And this hasty little note she sent the next day before she sailed :

"*November* 11.

"MY DEAR LOUISE: I seize this, my last opportunity of sending you a word. Will not you come and see me off? I suppose we will be at the steamer about half past one or two. Inclosed you will find *me*, [her photograph,] and, dear friend, in return give me your prayers, for I shall be tempted. May the merciful Father bless us both, and if fated to meet again no more on earth, I know we shall join hand in hand around the throne and eternally bless Him who died for us."

CHAPTER VII.

IN NEW ORLEANS.

" The path of the just is as the shining light, which shineth
more and more unto the perfect day."

IN the last chapter we parted with Mary as, in company with her uncle and cousins, Mr. Mason and
family, she bade adieu to the large company who
assembled to bid " good-by."   No marked inci
dents occurred during the pleasant voyage; but
the passengers will not soon forget the young
lady whose attractive appearance, sincere, hon-
est face, and discreet conduct, so contrasting
with the flippancy of others, won the admiration
and commanded the respect of all who beheld her.
During the few days her father subsequently spent
in New Orleans, he was addressed by different gentlemen, fellow-passengers with Mary, in words of
congratulation in being father to so noble a daughter.   They expressed themselves delighted to
have found one whose simplicity and naturalness,
purity and dignity, adorned her sex, and exalted

real womanhood, in the midst of society for the most part hollow and artificial. On arriving at New Orleans she became an inmate of the family of her cousins, (Mr. and Mrs. Brush,) whose kindness to the invalid rendered her absence from home so tolerable. Indeed, in such a pleasant home, with her uncle's family in the neighborhood, she could feel none of the isolation so often experienced by strangers in a strange land.

Her six months' career in that city is so clearly and graphically related by her temporary pastor, Rev. J. P. Newman, that his friendly memorial is appended without further introduction:

"Mary Elizabeth North was a beautiful example of the *Christian from home.* Coming to New Orleans in the autumn of 1863, she remained here until the spring of the succeeding year. The winter of '64 was remarkable for its universal gayety, and even dissipation. Under the false impression that the social evils incident to war might be alleviated by conviviality, and fraternal relations permanently restored by the sumptuous dinner and the merry dance, those high in authority presided at the former and led in the latter. Fast living was the order of the day, and extravagance ruled

the fashions. Fortunes were made in a day, and
squandered as soon. Away from the restraints of
home, men departed from the teachings of their
youth; and Christians, charmed with the prospect
of speedy wealth, and delighted with the 'pleasures of sin,' yielded to the allurements of the hour,
and in too many instances lost fortune, reputation,
and God. Young men, delirious with excitement,
abandoned themselves to sinful pleasures, and either
sank to infamy here, or returned to their northern
homes bereft of virtue, wrecks of better days.
Nor were women less susceptible of the baneful
influences of the times. They emulated their hus-
bands and brothers at the festive board, and rivaled
them in the intoxication of the waltz and quadrille.
To most of them it was a new life. Reared to
self-restraint, and to find their chief enjoyment in
deeds of charity and in acts of devotion, they suddenly found themselves in a city where worldly
enjoyments, inconsistent with personal piety, were
regarded the privilege rather than the dishonor of
the Christian. The night was wasted in merriment, the day was spent in languor. Night after
night, in masked attire, or fantastic costume, they
threaded the mazes of the dance, or sat delighted
in the opera and theater, or lingered long at the

convivial board, where the wine was 'red,' and
where not unfrequently the morning light found
them intensely engaged in games of chance. Such
was the moral state of New Orleans the half year
Miss North was here. It is no marvel that personal piety was at a discount, and that attending
church once on the Lord's day was deemed the
sum of religion. To live godly in such times was
to suffer persecution; but the marvel is how she
kept herself ' unspotted from the world.' Young,
beautiful, attractive, she was the recipient of numerous invitations to join the festive scene; but O
what steadfastness she displayed, what preferences
for the sweet rest of devotion, what proof that her
' conversation was in heaven!' Like Moses,
' choosing rather to suffer afflictions with the
people of God, than to enjoy the pleasures of
sin for a season; esteeming the reproach of
Christ greater riches than the treasures in Egypt,
for he had respect unto the recompense of the
reward.'

" Sweetly, quietly she contented herself with the
refined amenities of home, or mingled in such
social gatherings as were consistent with her profession, and permitted by her conscience

" Hers was a rare life that memorable winter.

She seemed alone in her choice, yet her very isolation made her attractive. Her influence soon began to be felt. Others were restrained in their extravagance and folly, and she became the center of a circle of refined social life, and to-day, while those who were ignorant of the principle which governed her, mourn their folly and weep over wasted fortunes, she is remembered with respect, and her pious memory is cherished with delight. I know of no truer, purer example of the constancy of a *Christian from home.* Whether the piety of too many is but a restraint, springing from self-respect or a desire for the esteem of friends and relatives, I know not; but it is patent to all that when among strangers men do many things contrary to their reputation at home, and which, if known, would exclude them from the communion of saints, and forfeit the favor of those by whom they are esteemed ; but her fidelity to Christ came from her simple, constant love for his name, and a wholesome fear of his displeasure. She was Christ's, and recognized the perpetuity of her obligations to him as to time, and their universality as to place.

"How much such decisions and devotions were due to early training and parental influence is best

evidenced by her almost constant references to
home. She had been trained up in the way she
should go, and did not depart therefrom, no, not
even among strangers. For every solicitation to
worldly pleasures she had some cherished saying
of father's, some remembered request of mother's. She lived as it were in their immediate presence. Memory brought them near, and in fancy
she was ever consulting the will of the one and the
wish of the other. She seemed never happier than
when describing some home scene, some feature of
family worship, some incident of parental govern-
ment, some peculiarity of father or mother, or re-
lating some story of domestic love. Her love of
home was unbounded. It was her delight to prepare tokens of affection for a sister or brother,
whose image she bore upon her heart while in a
distant land; and she was not unfrequently heard
to sing

> ' Do they miss me at home,
> Do they miss me ? '

To the song-question of a daughter so dutiful
and a sister so devoted, the response could only be
emphatic; and now since her flight from earth,
more than ever before, they miss her from home.

"Although truly and religiously select in the

choice of companionship, yet her piety was not morose, nor was she ascetic. Her young heart was gushing with affection, her spirit was elastic and joyous; her countenance evinced a contented mind, full of hope and promise. Her merry laugh still lingers in the ear of friendship, and her sweet maiden face still lights the memory of affection. Her judgment was mature beyond her years, and her mind was so evenly balanced that self-control and the control of others was seldom a task. More than once during her residence in New Orleans she displayed this power. One possessed of her personal charms could not be otherwise than attractive, and those who sought her hand were not a few; but disinclined to form an alliance, she embraced the opportunity to speak of Jesus, and the interview terminated with serious religious impressions.

"Nor was her piety inactive. Tenderly loving children, she accepted the charge of the infant class connected with the Sunday-school of the Felicity-street Methodist Episcopal Church. This was the sphere of her activities. Here all her tender solicitude was awakened, here her faith was the 'substance of things hoped for, and the evidence of things not seen.' And now, after an absence from us of more than a twelvemonth, the infant lips she taught to lisp a Saviour's praise speak a teacher's name. Her life will be reproduced in theirs; she lives in them. It was her happiness to be here when Bishop Ames visited the Crescent City to plant a loyal Church, and the writer remembers her interesting account of that great historic event published in one of our religious papers. That letter will form part of the written history of this mission. Not a small portion of it was devoted to the organization of the Sunday-school, evincing the interest she felt in that cause.

"Perhaps she never manifested during her whole life the true heroine more than when in the winter of '64 she engaged as a teacher in a negro Sunday-school. Her womanly heart yearned over a long despised and oppressed race, and casting aside the scorn of enemies and remonstrances of timid friends, she went forward, lifting up the fallen and making wise the simple. And now, since that inaugural labor, that day of small things, the children of Africa fill our day-schools and throng our churches on the Lord's day. They and we are now reaping the fruits of her labors; and her quiet, unostentatious work of love will not be forgotten when the Lord shall come to make up his jewels. 'Write,

Blessed are the dead which die in the Lord from henceforth; yea, saith the Spirit, that they may rest from their labors; and their works do follow them.'

" But there is another aspect of her character to be contemplated, and one other incident in her brief stay in our city to be related. It was during a period of great destitution among our troops, and especially the wounded here, that, moved by generous impulses, Mrs. Banks proposed a tableau entertainment for the benefit of such, and our departed friend appeared as Charity in the tableau of 'Faith, Hope, and Charity.' The object to be attained was no less worthy than the enjoyment afforded was refined. The immense building in which it was held was densely crowded with the intelligence, beauty, wealth, and soldiery of the city. Neither art nor expense had been spared to render the occasion a great success, and the proceeds therefrom not only met the full expectation of the originators of the plan, but relieved the wants of our brave but suffering soldiers. Each tableau was produced with exquisite taste and with no little elaboration, and each in turn received its well deserved meed of praise. But for simple, chaste, artless beauty, the "Tableau of the Three

Graces " was unexcelled. There stood Faith with
her cross, pure and ethereal; on her left was Hope,
radiant and joyful, holding fast the symbolic an-
chor; while on her right stood Charity, benign and
loving, to whose ample robes three children of
poverty clung, looking up into her sweet and
gentle face to find a response to their infant wants.
'And now abideth faith, hope, charity, these three;
but the greatest of these is charity.'"*

In addition to Dr. Newman's testimony the following incident is subjoined. Some months after
Mary's return from New Orleans her parents
planned a short trip for her, stopping on the way
in Philadelphia. While there a merchant who had
spent the winter in New Orleans called to pay his
respects to Mary. Taking the father aside, he said
substantially, "I wish to express my admiration
for your daughter, whose conduct was so noble
during her visit in New Orleans. Even we mar-
ried gentlemen found the fascination of the place a
severe ordeal for our consistency. The tendency
in every thing was downward. There was nothing
in religious or social influence strong enough to

* In this tableau Mrs. Newman was Faith, Mrs. Brush, Hope,
and Miss North, Charity.

hold men back from the whirlpool of sinful pleasure. But your daughter, placed in the midst of a circle of Northerners, held us all up. Her pure example and gentle admonitions strengthened our resolutions, and kept us from yielding to temptation. For myself, I owe her a debt of gratitude words cannot express."

We now turn with pleasure to a little package of letters written during this period, which show us Mary's inner life yet more fully. The first bears date

" Thanksgiving, 1863.

"Our passage out was very fine, the weather beautiful and clear nearly all the time, and O! the moonlight nights upon the sea. It would be no use for me to attempt to describe them, or my emotions while enjoying them; only I felt like holding my breath and praising Him.

"My first view of the city in detail was from the deck of the steamer, and in the distance on the wharf were seen two circuses in full operation, and this on Sunday! Ah me, I thought, what a wicked city!

"My cough is better, but not well; I doubt whether it ever will leave me entirely."

"*December* 8.

"I thank you, dear father, for your loving and interesting letter, which I received this morning. It was not my intention to write to you by this steamer, but the impulse to do so is irresistible, and most gladly do I obey it. Last Sabbath I went to the Baptist church twice; cousin Annie B. is delighted with the prospect of having a 'Union Methodist Church' in town, and she and I intend to hunt up Bishop Ames and see whether we can help him.

"Pa, do not throw away your talents in the pursuit of wealth, but think how much we will glory if at the day of reckoning Christ will award such words to you, 'Well done, good and faithful servant.' Have you ever tried to imagine what your emotions would be when standing before the throne, and receiving words of commendation from the lips of Him whom we adore?

"This city is a hard place to be good in, but 'Lead me not into temptation,' is my daily prayer. I hope to pass through the furnace of exposure and trial without so much as a hair of my head singed, or the smell of sin upon my garments. God bless and keep us evermore.

"Ever your own　　　　　　　　"MARY."

" December 11.

"The Friday after I came here a young lady spent the day with us, and a little more than a week after we attended her funeral. She was taken, Saturday morning, with a congestive chill, and in thirty-six hours she died—died the day she was nineteen.

"The deaths in this climate are so sudden that we fear and tremble from day to day. But the same great Love that has brought me here will take me safely home; such is my faith. My heart sinks with shame when I remember the small return I make for this ocean of love divine. 'Tis even as one has said: 'Thy love has been as a shower, the return but a dew-drop, and that dew-drop stained by sin.'

"This city is perfectly terrible with its wickea ness; there is no regard for the Sabbath, and balls and theaters seem to be attended on that day in preference to another.

"I should not be at all surprised if I remained here all winter, for my cough has improved but little, and this week I received word from pa to remain until he sent more explicit word, unless I was quite well. My mother seems rather poorly all the time, and that troubles me, for you know a daughter's yearning over a sick mother burdened with cares.

"God bless you, my friend."

"*December* 26.

"Another aged one passed into eternity! Another tie to bind you there. 'O say, will you go to the Eden above?' Louise, it may be that I will reach that happy place before you; the future is vailed from our view; but I have a yearning, O so deep! to be perfectly good, and it can only be secured in heaven. Never before has strength from above been more needed by me than now, and it seems as if—yes, I am sure I never felt that strength so great as I do now. O if I only can do good! Example will speak louder than words here; I want to be like an anagram, read up and down, and all ways the same—no inconsistency.

"Some of my friends are trying to persuade me to go to the opera, and they insist that it will not hurt me. But the more they insist, so much the more I am determined *not* to go. My conscience condemns the amusement as sinful, and though I would give anything to hear the music *if* it was right, yet I will not go.

"We enjoyed our Christmas very well, though

all our company were strangers in a strange land. How strange it must have seemed at home to have no Mary, no Charlie, and more than likely no father, for I hope to see pa here by Sunday or next day.

"May a happy New Year be yours!"

"*January* 2, 1864.

"DEAREST CHARLIE: You know as well as I how many things we have to praise God for in reviewing 1863. I hope, and shall try with all the powers given me, to exert an influence for good wherever I go; and I do hope that some good may come of my stay here.

"As yet I have not identified myself with any particular Sunday-school, but think I will help Mrs. H. in one for colored children. So imagine your brilliant sister busily engaged in teaching colored ideas how to find the way to heaven.

"Have you ever carefully read the nineteenth Psalm, especially the last four verses: 'Who can understand his errors? Cleanse Thou me from secret faults. Let the words of my mouth, and the meditation of my heart, be acceptable in thy sight, O Lord, my strength and my redeemer.'"

" January 15.

"It is decided that New Orleans is to be my home until May. I've been here two months, and the days have passed 'as a tale that is told.' My cough is abating, and under the blessing of a kind Father I hope to be well ere long.

" My love to all, and God bless you."

" January 22.

" DEAR CHARLIE : I believe God will make me the means of doing some good; at least, all here seem to have the impression that I am a Christian girl, and O! may the Lord help me to maintain a consistent Christian character. There is the rub— inconsistency.

" Well, with a strong reliance on my kind Father in heaven, I feel ready to battle with the world, the flesh, and the devil."

" January 30.

" What a blessed thing that the Holy Spirit is adapted to every want and every phase of experi ence. I have often realized it, and so have you.

" I have been reading a book that uncle gave me on Christmas, entitled 'The Corner-Stone,' by Jacob Abbott, in which he discusses the principal features of our Saviour's character; and especially this :

'Who, when he was reviled, reviled not again.'
About his Father's business, he was bold, courage-
ous, persevering; but as soon as he himself was in-
jured it was of so little moment that he passed by it
with scarcely a thought. I never before realized
so clearly the difference between the two points.

"You ask me if I do not think that we increase
in favor of man, if we do with God. No. I think
not always; for gaining higher favor with God, it
necessarily follows that our pursuits and tastes will
differ from the majority of the world's, and there
will arise unkind remarks about self-righteousness,
etc.; but in the end man's admiration and respect
will be gained, don't you think so, Louise? Even
the most depraved cannot but respect a real good
person.

"Wednesday evening we went to call on Mrs.
General Banks, but she was out, so we spent the
evening with a friend of Annie's. Yesterday we
were all invited out to dinner. To-night we are
going to a concert, so you see our time is pretty
well occupied either with company or going out.
I like it very well; but the thought comes, Am I
doing any good? But a silent influence for good
cannot but emanate from me if I am pure and
holy."

To Miss P., who was residing in New Orleans:

"*February* 1.

"Did you enjoy yesterday? It was a pretty busy day with me. The children and I, by dint of great exertion, started off for Sunday-school in F-street; we wended our way until we reached the church. Sublime disorder reigned within the school-room, in strange contrast with the sweet Sabbath peace without. You know how lovely it all was, the bright sunshine and the balmy, delicious air breathing a blessing directly upon us from our Father. I felt so happy and peaceful, for I knew that my Saviour looked down and smiled.

"The school, I hope, will be improved in a few Sundays when we get fairly established. The infant class may be my position, and if so, God help me to do them some good. My litle colored scholars amuse me, and at the same time I like to teach them, they are so bright, and make such comical remarks.

"May God help us both to fill up the measure of our existence with good deeds and holy influences, and in his own good time take us *home* to himself. O what exquisite pleasure in this idea and certainty of perfect rest! Yours ever."

The following was found after Mary's death in her portfolio:

"New Orleans, *February* 13, 1864.

"How strange! Nearly three months since I left home, and how has it fared with me since then? Have I the same guileless trusting heart that was within me when I came? Much more of worldly experience has been mine during these three months than ever before, and can I say truly that the world has left no taint upon me? Heavenly Father, thou knowest that I am passing through the furnace! but beside me there is one having the form of the Son of God, and gently but firmly upheld by him, my garments will not have so much as the smell of sin upon them. O keep me, for I am very weak; but thou hast said, 'He will give his angels charge over thee, to keep thee in all thy ways; and in their hands they shall bear thee up, lest thou dash thy foot against a stone.' I come to-night into my closet, where no eye can see, and dare to claim an interview with thee, Father of light and life. O my Saviour, meet me, and take this poor doubting sinful heart, and tenderly pour the balm of Gilead upon it. Remove everything that may in any way interfere with thy supremacy there, even the dearest of earthly affection, if need be.　But O Father, is there a 'need-be?'　Cannot I yield to the siren's power without sinning!　No, no, I cannot, I must not; for how could I stand at the bar of God and plead not guilty?　O Father, take the heart which, with humble faith, I cast upon thee, and cleanse its depths from all impurity for my Redeemer's sake.

"To-morrow will be the holy Sabbath; early in the morning I must rise and prepare my two darlings and myself for Sabbath-school, and may the Lord in mercy aid me in imparting instruction to the little ones who look so trustingly upon me.　O my Father, grant me a blessing this night!　Amen."

"New Orleans, February 19.

"Dear Cousin Annie : For some weeks after I came it was so undecided whether I should remain or not, that I did not like to engage in a Sunday-school, for fear I should have to give it up right away; but now the Sabbath is my busiest day.　In the morning the two children and myself start for our own school, and there I have charge of the in-fant class, numbering about thirty, until eleven o'clock, when we go to church and remain there till half past twelve.　At a quarter of one I go to a colored Sunday-school, and teach a class of near-ly twenty.　So in all there are about fifty children spiritually under my care. Have you ever noticed in the 'Sunday-School Bell' a hymn called 'The Teacher's Prayer,' beginning

'Save all my children, Lord?'

That is just the way I feel, and especially here, where I have to act alone, with no father nor mother to advise me. If ever I needed grace, it is now, and how glad I am to say it is given. I often think of this: that it is not so much what we actually *do* for God that tells whether we are true Christians, as what we *are*. Religion must be interwoven with the very essence of our being, so that every thought, word, and action will bear its impress. Annie, dear, are we each as holy as we ought to be, when we remember how we have been brought up in the very lap of religion?"

"*February* 19.

"Dear Florence: I believe a merciful Father whom we both love, and whose we are, will let me live to return home.

"Did you ever think of the Bible representation of the love existing between David and Jonathan, which surpassed the love of women? Do you not take it, *that* is considered the highest type of affection?

10

"Do you not find that you tire easily of these mere worldly pleasures? How poorly the soul would thrive if it had no better nor stronger food. Would there be any need of a heaven if we possessed no higher capacity for enjoyment than mere physical pleasure? I do not believe there would, for this earth would be heaven enough.

"I have real nice times on Sunday teaching in two schools, having charge of about fifty children. I am so much happier with a large work to do."

"*March* 4.

"LOUISE: I sometimes don't know what to make of myself; I cannot tell whether it is want of interest or great peace which I experience, for most of the time there is no great fear or consciousness of sin, and I always try to have my motives pure and truthful, and to be guided by the word of God.

"Father in heaven! help me to be thy faithful, true child, and forgive all my sins.

"Your image is often with me when I pray; I wonder whether our souls meet in such an hour."

"*March* 11.

"O this glorious South, with its never-fading flowers and its sunny skies! Every thing is full of impulse, and done with all its might, but no stability.

"Day before yesterday it threatened rain in the morning, and before long the drops came, not cool and calculating like northern drops, but rushing headlong, pell-mell, and in two hours there was not a stepping-place but was covered with nearly a foot of water. It seemed as if a crevasse had visited the city, and we might easily have sailed through some of the streets in a flat-bottomed boat. I never saw anything equal to it in my life. And when the sun shines, it is with a strength that reminds you of haymaking in the hottest day of August.

"The gardens are gloriously beautiful now, teeming with vegetation and beauty. Every letter that I write to the North contains a few mad rhapsodies about the 'bright weather and the flowers; but I cannot help it, for when I write my seat is by a window that overlooks our beautiful garden, and the influence or inspiration of it fills my whole soul, and my only safety-valve is in writing.

"This winter has been a pleasant and peaceful one, though the experiences of course have been entirely new. I have seen and mingled a great

deal more with the world, and I tell you, not
boastingly but thankfully, that the desire to deal
entirely with pure and holy things is more intense
than ever.   It is harder to be good, because the
temptation sometimes seems too strong to be re-
sisted; but, thanks to a Christian training, I know
where to go and freely draw new supplies of grace.

"Teaching in Sabbath-school is a great pleasure;
when I see the dear children's faces turned so
lovingly to me as their teacher, surely the reward
would be sufficient, even without the consciousness
that our Father in heaven approved."

"*March* 11.

"Do you ever wonder what work God has for
you to do? Is your conviction still strong that
you ought to enter the ministry? Sometimes it
seems to me that God must have some great work
for me to do, because my happiness up to this time
has been almost uninterrupted, and it cannot be
that it will always continue so without some particular end in view.

"Sometimes I long to plunge into something
decided, but I know this—the greatest achieve-
ments are more frequently in quiet life, and over
little things; so let patience have her perfect work
in me."

" *March* 17.

" What a grand sublime sight is old ocean, and
how intense the feeling of one's own helplessness
and insignificance compared with the mighty power
of that great body of water. I used to sit and
watch the waves chasing each other, and the ever-
restless waters lashing themselves furiously against
the ship's side, as if incensed at the temerity of
man in attempting to force his vessel through
them. And I felt how great was the care of a
mindful Father in preserving us in the midst of so
much danger. On viewing the sunrise at sea, I
could realize more than I ever did how ' God said,
" Let there be light," and there was light.'

" But, Ella, we enjoyed the most enchanting
moonlight evenings that one could conceive. The
evening we stopped at Havana gave me a better
idea than I ever had before of the beauty of that
comparison in which a soul at perfect peace is
' calm as summer evenings be.' "

" *March* 17.

" I am very happy in one sense of the word;
never was looking better; my cough is pretty well
cured; I am surrounded by the dearest of friends,
and more than all, Florence, the greatest of friends
is mine. My Father and yours owns and blesses

me and calls me his child.   These lines will run in
my mind the whole time I am writing to you.

> "'Tis not the whole of life to live,
> Nor all of death to die.'

I do not know what reminds me of them, but do
you ever think of them?   What object would
there be in living if life closed when the spirit left
the body?   No, we only fairly begin to live when
the River of Death is crossed.   O, think of the
countless ages which lie before the new-born soul!
and do you not think that each successive age in
the spirit-world will find us more sanctified and
etherealized, so that there is a nearer approach to
Deity?   Or is the progress all made in this world,
and when once launched into eternity do we remain non-progressive, but of course in a state of
perfect bliss compared with this earth?"

"*March* 25.

"DEAR LOUISE: I feel perfectly forlorn this
morning, sick, weak, and, worse than all, homesick.   I have been quite well and improving nicely,
but unfortunately on Sunday last I took a severe
cold, which has settled all over me, and now my
cough is just as bad as ever.   Sometimes it seems
as if I had been committing some dreadful wicked-

ness, for which this hateful cough has been sent as
a punishment; what specially I cannot see, but
there is a 'need-be' in it, and although I may
never know the reason, yet my kind Father knows
what is best for his erring child. It is my firm
conviction that I never will be well of this trouble;
I may and do get better, but not entirely.

"How any one can prefer the belief of the anni-
hilation of the soul to its transformation and puri-
fication, seems wonderful. If I could feel a perfect
certainty of my reward hereafter, care might be
increased tenfold, and still it would be borne.
How I like this little chant:

> 'Nearer, my God, to thee,
>   Nearer to thee;
> Even though it be a cross that raiseth me,
>   Still all my song shall be
> Nearer my God to thee, nearer to thee.'

"So another of our friends has gone to rest, Mr.
B. We'll meet in heaven. O, Louise, do you feel
afraid to die? I do not; if the Lord should call
me this night my soul would respond, 'Even so,
Lord Jesus, come quickly.'

"Our friends, Messrs. K. and S., and H., who
have been very kind to us this winter, left New
Orleans last Saturday in the 'Evening Star' for

home. It makes me so impatient and homesick to see others going, and to think that my turn is not come yet.

"Remember me to all, and God bless us both. Yours ever."

"*April* 1, 1864.

"MY DARLING BROTHER: What a beautiful relation is that existing between brother and sister. Have you ever thought that the whole glorified Church above will bear this same relation? for there is neither marrying nor giving in marriage, and God will be our Father, and Christ our elder Brother. So it seems to me that our relation is one of the most sanctified.

"O may the Lord bless and keep my precious brother is my daily prayer!"

About the last of April Mary bade adieu to her friends in New Orleans, and took passage for home in a sailing vessel. This was recommended in preference to a steamer, as giving a longer voyage, which it was fondly hoped would complete her restoration to health. The only record which remains to us of her life during the voyage is the subjoined letter to her mother, written by a lady whose acquaintance with Mary was begun on board the "Winthrop:"

"My Dear Mrs. N.: Although we started strangers on our journey homeward from the South, I gained an insight into Mary's character which only such an intimate mode of living as one experiences on shipboard could so soon give. From the first I was impressed with the sincerity of her Christian principles, and I ever felt that of her it could truly be said she 'let her light shine before men.' She hesitated not, when opportunity offered, to speak of her hope as a Christian, and to recommend religion to others by her words and actions.

" The trip at sea she enjoyed with all the childish enthusiasm of her nature, saying her spirit knew no bound to its delight. She would pace the deck by hours during the day, and when reclining at evening beneath the star-studded heavens, contemplating the works of the great Divine, she would talk of his infinite power and love, and the duty of Christians to live above earth's fleeting joys, trying to impress others with the value of Christian living.

"At one time, being grieved at the profanity among 'he officers of the ship, she went directly to the captain, and spoke to him in a kindly reproving tone on the subject; nor did her honesty of purpose and gentleness fail to have their effect.

On several occasions, in order to pass away the time pleasantly and profitably, we held Bible-class meetings among the few passengers, when Mary's knowledge of the Scriptures, in her ever-ready replies and references, proved that she was no stranger to its teachings, nor had she idly read the word of God.

"Very often would she speak with tender affection of her parents, and each member of the dear, happy home circle, rejoicing that so many had in early life been gathered into the Saviour's fold.

"For her kindness in the wearisome hours of illness that were appointed to me, I cannot express my gratitude, for she constantly ministered to my wants, and watched with tender sisterly anxiety my every need till we reached our homes.

"A strange Providence it seems that I, who then lay at death's door, should have been restored to health, while she, so much better during the voyage, should so soon have passed away, the anniversary of our arrival in New York being the day of her death; but He doeth all things well. Her mission was ended; she had finished the work her Father gave her to do, and she has been called to receive her reward. Though dead, she yet speaketh to us by her holy living and holy dying. God grant that we, too, may die the death of the righteous.

"Believe me your sincerely sympathizing friend,

"SOPHIE B."

And thus ends the simple story of a six months' away from home. The story *is* simple; but who can tell of the doubts and fears which troubled our Mary, when enfeebled in body and yearning for home and parents to protect and advise her. Her path was beset with temptations, flowery byways were open to her, and siren voices bade her enter with safety. But how simply she tells it, "I knew where to go for help and it never failed me." Truly the Lord was on her side, and they that were for her were more than all they that were against her.

My young friend, have you chosen the Lord for your portion? Have you set him on your right hand, so that you shall not be moved? "There are but two really happy states in this world, either that of the man who rejoices in the light of God's countenance, or that of him who mourns after it." Is yours the first? Have you tasted and seen that the Lord is good? O then be diligent; the time is short; bury not your talent in a napkin; be faithful in the least, and great shall be your reward.   But perhaps yours is the state of the man who mourns after the favor of God.   O, rest not in all the plain till the appointed place be found where God shall bless you, and lift upon you the light of his countenance.

We have sometimes almost regretted that so many of Mary's last days were spent away from us; but if good was done by her precept and example, and if this memorial of her useful life shall lead one soul to the foot of the Lord, we can but rejoice.

> " And when that happy time shall come,
>   Of endless peace and rest,
> We shall look back upon our path,
>   And say it was the best."

CHAPTER VIII.

THE INVALID.

Now I saw in my dream, that by this time the pilgrims were got over the Enchanted Ground, and entering into the country of Beulah, whose air was very sweet and pleasant. The way lying directly through it, they solaced themselves there for a season. In this country the sun shineth night and day: wherefore this was beyond the Valley of the Shadow of Death, and also out of the reach of Giant Despair; neither could they from this place so much as see Doubting Castle.—BUNYAN.

" ASHRIDGE, *May* 16.

"HOME at last, and O the joy of being here among those whom I can call my own! On Saturday morning I arrived safely in port, thanks to a kind Providence. Our trip home was very propitious until the last two days. O, Florence, it is utterly impossible to express what one feels when surrounded by such an expanse of water, heaving and surging, ever restless; and at night 'the heavens declare the glory of God, and the firmament showeth his handiwork.' 'Who is like unto thee, O Lord, among the gods? Who is like unto thee, glorious in holiness, fearful in praises, doing wonders?' When I used to look on the stars at night,

and gaze into their depths until my soul was lost
in wonder, sweetly would come over my being the
influence of the 'Star of Bethlehem.'

'One star alone the Saviour speaks,
It is the Star of Bethlehem.'''

"Ashridge, *May* 30.

"Dear Cousin Annie: *Home at last!* Joy!
joy! It is really and truly so, that this child is at
home. I have not the least difficulty in feeling the
influence of home; it makes me so happy and light-
hearted once more to feel secure in this haven of
rest, this refuge from sin. Two weeks ago last
Saturday I arrived in New York.

"The same beneficent Hand that has guided me
safely through life thus far, gave us favorable
winds and quiet seas, and on the morning of the
sixteenth day we anchored in the harbor with the
sunlight shining clear. Dangers of the worst kind
had beset our little vessel; privateers in the Gulf,
and one night in a squall our mizzen-topmast was
snapped right off. Yet in the midst of all the
Saviour walked, and 'Peace, be still,' hushed every
fear.

"The most exquisite happiness filled my soul as
I stood by the bulwarks of the vessel and looked

at the white crested heaving waters, eternally restless, and then turning my gaze upward beheld the heavens dark with clouds; but through them all I saw a star—it was the star of Bethlehem. And O! Annie, the thought that the Creator of all that sublimity was my Father, gave me such perfect trust and peace that I never felt the slightest fear.

" When I stepped suddenly in the 'office,' and my father, who was not expecting me that day, suddenly spied his rosy sailor-girl, the ' Why, my daughter!' and embrace which followed proved the depth of his love. And when the carriage brought me to the door of *home* the scene beggars description. The children performed wonderful evolutions; ma and I cried; and, O dear! I knew that I was truly welcome. Yours ever."

Mary's story of her home-coming is more interesting than any other's narrative, as showing her feelings of joy and thankfulness; but a little incident which her father will never forget may find place here. As she entered her father's office on the morning of her arrival, after the first greeting he led her to a seat in a more private room, when, looking up in his face with an expression of serene satisfaction, she said, "Pa, I have returned to you just as pure as when I left home; I am the same Mary."

As soon as the first excitement of return was over Mary engaged in her wonted home duties, which had been interrupted by her previous ill health. The joy of the family was great at having their loved one restored to them, almost recovered; but, alas! they marked not that the rose-tint on her cheek was deeper than that of perfect health; that her form grew thinner, and her step lighter and slower. The cough, to which all were now so much accustomed, seemed to change its character; and almost insensibly it came to be not uncommon that sister's seat at breakfast would be vacant, and that the children should play quietly while Mary lay down after dinner. One little feature, however, could not remain unnoticed: that one voice was no more heard in the song of praise at family worship, for Mary's cough debarred her from singing. Still we could not think that she was to leave us. Grown doubly dear since a short separation, how could we bear to dream of a long farewell!

So in working, sewing, and entertaining friends; in sweet home pleasures and innocent enjoyments, the summer days glided swiftly by. Ah, little did we then think how precious their memory would shortly be to us!

During this summer Mary enjoyed much horse-back exercise; she had always been fond of it, and while in the South rode as often as circumstances would permit; but now returned to Romeo and her own loved hills, with one of her brothers for escort, who so earnestly entered into the sport as Mary? She and the pony understood each other perfectly, and although restless and troublesome with others, he was gentle and obedient to her. When other members of the family were out for a drive, she would frequently accompany the carriage on Romeo; and when the ground was level enough to admit of it, she would start off as on the wings of the wind, and one could hardly tell which was most exhilarated, the horse or his rider. The picture of the beautiful young lady on the white pony will long remain in the memory of the inhabitants of Scarborough and its vicinity.

To Mary's letters again we turn, and find every line a mirror of herself. The first is to the friend who has written so lovingly of their intimacy on the voyage home.

11

"Ashbridge, *June* 10.

"My dear Sophie : We are not rich, but every needful luxury is supplied, and our home is made the happiest place on earth by our parents' love. Such a home is specially needed when there are so many boys. We have five, and we thank God the three older ones were safely inclosed within the Church's protection when very young. The other two are babies yet, being the youngest of the family.

"How hard it is to do right so that no stumbling-block may stand in the way of those dear brothers. But the source from whence all help comes is all-sufficient, and working through Christ, who strengtheneth me, I pray that the end may prove that my life has not been spent in vain. My heavenly Father knows that the most intense desire of my heart is to live uprightly. But, dear Sophie, I fear you will deem me egotistical to write so much of myself and our family. But you are an older sister, and have felt the same.

"May our kind Father speedily restore you to perfect health; and may the peace that passeth all understanding keep you and abide with you ever.

"Your friend   "Mary."

"ASHRIDGE, *June* 29.

"The month has passed very pleasantly since I've been home. You may imagine how busy the sewing, working, entertaining company, and thousand and one things which an oldest daughter finds to do, have kept me.

" O, Florence, home is so pleasant! Pa has made many improvements on the place, and then there is that eternal source of beauty, the ever-flowing river, which to both of us will be 'a joy forever.'

" Two flowers in full bloom have been transplanted from among your choice collection to the banks of the River of Life. Were they beautifully fragrant with the love of Christ, or though perfect in form, lacked they the ' one thing needful ? '

" Our plants have been despoiled of their perfect numbers by the great Pruner. Uncle Frank's little darling sleeps quietly in one of the Saviour's conservatories; but its essence, or life, is safely preserved on high, awaiting the resurrection morn, when corruptible shall put on incorruption, and bloom in the glory of midsummer beauty."

The following is to the same aged friend to whom Mary wrote once before going to New Orleans:

"*July* 27.

"Dear Mrs. F.: If every action of your life resulted in as much good as your last letter has done me, how great will be your reward. Like water to a thirsty land, (which has been so forcibly impressed upon us recently,) so were your words of comfort and advice to my soul.

"On Saturday last we returned from Middletown, after having enjoyed a few days of unalloyed happiness. The commencement exercises were rather more interesting than two years since, or else I appreciated them better. In fact, almost everything that has occurred since my return home from the South has possessed a double interest in me. There is nothing in the world that renders home, and the thousand interests and circumstances connected with it, so valuable as the deprivation of them for a season. I never wish to leave-home again unless accompanied by some of its members.

"How can any one have any other aim in life than that of doing good, and living in such a manner as will be acceptable to our heavenly Father? Sometimes I fear that my anxiety to know the future becomes sinful. It seems as though there were latent powers within me struggling for exercise, and as yet nothing has drawn them out; but ' what wilt Thou have me to do?' is my daily cry. Is it wrong, is it sinful for me to feel thus, or must these indefinite longings for something higher and nobler be stifled? Is it not strange that we are not more earnest in our endeavors to become more holy and purified? The great error of my own life has been too great confidence in my own strength. I had thought, and tried to believe, that my reliance was entirely upon divine strength; but my merciful Father has opened my eyes, and shown me my weakness, and why in many cases, where I thought nothing could move me, I have slipped. And now with great trembling I live day by day, continually praying, 'Give me strength to live aright.' You say you hope to precede me to 'the better land.' O, Mrs. F., I almost doubt whether you will do so; strange misgivings fill my heart; I should not be at all surprised if the Lord took me first. I have the forerunner of disease upon me, and though there is no present danger, still unless I can speedily be cured, these robes of corruption will soon be exchanged for those pure and holy ones in which I can see my Redeemer face to face.

'How I long to be there, and its glories to share,
    And to lean on my Saviour's breast!'

"Do not be alarmed by what I have said. My general health is good, and my cough much abated since my return home, and mother trusts to a strong constitution, aided by medicine, to conquer it entirely.

"It fills me with gladness to know that your health is so good at present; may the Lord continue it so!

"May the Lord keep and preserve you, and grant you the riches of his grace.

"YOUR YOUNG FRIEND."

"*July 27.*

"And, Louise, the fact is, I feel very different now compared to former experiences. My confidence in myself is all gone, I trust; and now I look up and say, 'Help, Lord, for I am poor and needy.' The desire to be purified from the slightest dross of evil grows more intense every hour. An aunt of mine has been visiting us, and she gave it as her opinion that my days on earth were almost numbered. I feel little faith in such predictions, but you know they must necessarily make me more thoughtful. Sometimes 'the blues' deal rather heavily with me, and it is all I can do to wear a cheerful countenance; but if the Lord wills that my stay upon earth be short, I will be the last one to murmur at his righteous dispensations. Mrs. F. wrote me such a beautiful letter last week, full of Christian counsel and saintly experience. I have been answering it this morning.

"God bless you, my dear friend."

Writing to her friend Florence, and referring to a recent affliction, she says:

"It may be that your heart was not wholly given up to its rightful Lord; and lest you should set up another object of worship in opposition to him, this affliction has been sent upon you. O, Florence, the Lord grant that you may become as refined as silver, pure and holy under the awful scrutiny of an Omniscient Father.

"Though the practice of writing ordinary letters on Sunday is decidedly wrong, still in such as this there surely can be no harm. Now while I am writing, the sweet sounds of the piano and flute come floating on the Sabbath evening air, a faint reminder of that never-ending rest, where we shall on psaltery and harp ceaselessly praise our risen Lord and Christ. O to be faithful unto death! so that we may receive a crown of life. And you and I will walk hand in hand on the banks of the River of Life. clad in garments made

white through the blood of our crucified Redeemer.
O, Florence, can it be that such everlasting blessedness is in store for us?"

"*August* 16.

"Never, indeed, has a summer passed so pleasantly and, I trust, profitably. I look around on my
happy home and my kind indulgent parents, and
come to this conclusion : that no young lady ever
had more to be thankful for than myself. And the
fact of my unworthiness inspires within me an in·
tense desire to devote all my energies toward a
useful life, and so I will, God helping me."

"*August* 20.

" O how lovely is this evening! I am sitting by
the front window, where I can see the beautiful
sunset exhibiting in its brilliant colors the handiwork of God. 'When I consider thy heavens, the
work of thy fingers, the moon and stars which thou
hast ordained, what is man, that thou art mindful of
him, and the son of man that thou visitest him? for
thou hast made him a little lower than the angels,
and hast crowned him with glory and honor.' I
think we too often forget the great honor our
heavenly Father has conferred upon us as his children and heirs—'heirs of God, and joint heirs with

our Lord Jesus Christ.' If we fully realized the responsibility resting upon us as such, the sense of it would be an additional restraint against sin. O Lord, make us thine own children, thy righteous, holy daughters!

"While on the camp-ground I attended a meeting where the definite object prayed for was holiness. And O how I prayed that self might be entirely immolated, and Christ and his will reign supreme! And I was blessed in a measure, thanks be unto him."

"*August* 81.

"MY DEAR MRS. F.: This summer has been one of the most pleasant that we have ever passed; such is the verdict of the whole family. My father's business has been greatly prospered, so that every reasonable wish has been gratified; then we have taken much pleasure in the society of many dear friends who have visited our home.

"We children have had such nice time riding. Romeo is doing finely, and we believe will carry his gray hairs with honor to the grave. He is full of life and spirits, and though sometimes a little headstrong, yet when his mistress is on his back a due sense of his responsibility comes over him, and he behaves accordingly. We all love Romeo so much that pa says he will keep him as long as he lives, and when he dies bury him with honors.*

"Surely no family ever had greater cause for thankfulness than we have, and we do all try to evince our gratitude to God by living godly lives; but O we so often fail.

"During camp-meeting I remained on the ground one day and attended a prayer-meeting for the promotion of holiness. If no one else was benefited I know that I was, in this way, that never before had I experienced such an intense longing to be perfect and pure in the eyes of a pure and holy God; and ever since I have been trying in God's strength to overcome self, and happily have succeeded in such a degree as has served to encourage my poor weak heart. You cannot tell how much I longed to see you just about that time; it seemed as if a conversation with one so experienced as yourself would be such a comfort.

"Your child in Christ,   "MARY."

"*August* 31.

"MY DEAR COUSIN: I suppose I must begin with the weather, that universal topic upon which

* Poor Romeo died one Sabbath morning within a year after his mistress.

the most illiterate are posted. Well, then, for the last two or three days it has been like September. How softly pure and cool the air is! the sky and water so blue, and clouds so white, and everything looking grandly clear, and proclaiming 'God is everywhere.' O, Annie, how you would enjoy it! I think we who are Christians can appreciate nature more fully than others, for we can trace a loving Father's hand in all things. Have you ever thought, in looking at a bunch of flowers, how many ideas of perfect beauty the Creator must have? Then pass from the vegetable king-dom to the animal, let your thought dwell on your own wonderful frame, and you will exclaim, 'I am fearfully and wonderfully made!' and finally turn your eyes to the starry heavens and ponder the countless millions contained in the almost invisible nebulæ; we can all say, 'Great and manifold are thy works, O Lord! in wisdom hast thou made them all!'"

In a letter written in September she says: "How inexpressible it makes me feel to view God proclaimed in all his works. I see him in the hills, in the river, in everything. I feel, I think like David when he said, 'When I consider thy heavens, the work of thy fingers, what is man?'

"Let us use for our motto 'the promotion of good within ourselves, and the advancement of God's glory.' We may prove to the world examples of truth and fidelity, which will result in the salvation of some precious soul, and I know that you will strive with me unto this end."

"September 4.

"I trust, dear Florence, that this has been a peaceful, happy day for you, and that the blessings of God's bountiful hand have rested on you in abundant measure. Sweetly and busily has the day passed with me: busily in performing the duties of daughter, nurse, and housekeeper; and sweetly in the enjoyment of a great measure of that 'perfect peace' and the consciousness of sins forgiven, and trying to do right."

"September 12.

"You ought to use your influence to its utmost extent, for a word spoken in season may save a soul from death. I read a very pretty story the other day, of a young lady who gave a bookmark with a verse of Scripture on it to an ungodly man, and made him promise that it should no remain two days in the same place in his Bible. The result was, the Lord converted him from the error of his ways, and a revival of religion began, which was the means of bringing many into the fold of Christ.

"O, my dear brother, try so to live that your most secret thoughts and actions might be exposed without your being ashamed of them! But how few of us would be willing to submit to such an ordeal!"

"*September* 24.

"It is Saturday afternoon, the closing hours of another week, and I think it will be well closed, my dear friend, if I spend the time in a chat with you. I can hardly express the anxiety we have all felt for you since my return from visiting your sick-bed. It was a great disappointment to me to leave you so soon, but I could not see my way clear to remain any longer. To have staid with you, and nursed you as best I knew how, would have given me much pleasure. When I think of your dear face worn by sickness, yet smiling so gently on your loved ones, it is impossible to restrain the ache in my heart when the possibility of losing you flashes over me; but I hope you are quite well again, and that you will soon feel your accustomed strength.

"It is very pleasant to leave home for a little time, and on returning be as heartily welcomed as Lila and I were. What dear loving parents we have, they take so much pleasure and interest in everything that concerns their children. Among my acquaintances I know one gentleman who wonders why his children act so contrary, and take so little interest in his wishes. Why, I believe he never went out with them, or tried to adapt himself to their capacities. How can he expect them to be as perfect and high-minded as he would desire, when he has taken so little personal interest in them? I thank God that we have had such good parents.

"It has been so warm that the gentle patter of the rain this afternoon sounds very refreshing. The river, the hills beyond, the whole landscape is enveloped in clouds; but far away there is a break in the dullness, with just enough blue sky to remind us that 'at evening time it shall be light.' How many sources of pleasure a Christian has in nature and her wonderful changes! Some think this autumn season is so very melancholy, the saddest of the year; but to me it seems a time of ripeness or fullness, for then the finest fruits are gathered, and the season of hard labor is over. So a child of God, just in that state before he rests from his labors, is ripe in all the Christian graces, and ready for the enjoyment of heaven.

"May every consolation which is afforded a needy, trusting soul be yours. I fervently thank God that he has granted you, according to his grace, to know the riches which his love contains, and that you so cheerfully abide his will.

"Your loving   "MARY."

"*October* 4.

"DEAR CHARLIE: Your last letter has been read and reread with such joy. Bless the Lord that you have such a heaven below. May the same blessings be ever yours, so that, alike in prosperity or adversity, 'Jesus all the day long will be your joy and your song.'"

Mary's father and mother had determined to spend the winter in the city, and arrangements were accordingly made for leaving Ashridge about the beginning of November. But the chilly winds of October began to have their effect on Mary's tender frame, and as her health commenced *visibly* to decline, the necessary preparations were hastened, that the family might be comfortably established before the winter had fairly set in. Still hopeful, for her trust and firm confidence was in the Lord, Mary assisted as much as possible with thoughtful suggestions, and willing, though feeble hands. So the middle of October found the whole family, with the exception of the absent student, fairly settled for the winter with a Christian family in New York. The first object now to be labored for was the restoration of Mary's health, and the second was the education of the boys.

Though prohibited by her physician from attending crowded meetings, going out in the night air, or exposing herself in the slightest degree, Mary made herself, O so happy at home. Naturally of a cheerful disposition, by the power of divine grace she had hitherto been able, even in hours of weakness and suffering, to maintain that command of herself which had won the admiration of all; but disease had now so enfeebled her whole frame, that it became a daily self-denial and cross-bearing to preserve that equanimity of temper and serenity of mind which had always been so characteristically her own. True, she had her moments of despondency and sadness as the thought would come that her "sickness was unto death;" but her manner in the family was so cheerful that few knew of the heart-struggles in her hours of retirement; and those who admired her lovely uncomplaining spirit, thought not of the weary night-watches, when, unable to sleep, she tossed from side to side, praying for patience, and pleading for strength to do and suffer all her heavenly Father's will.

In a few letters written at the time she speaks freely of her hopes and fears:

" October 26.

" I am prohibited from going out this winter to any place where it will be crowded, even church ; so books will be my principal recreation. I am feeling pretty well the last few days, and am very much encouraged. Surely the prayers of my many friends will be answered. We are happily situated as a family, and ought to do a great deal of good."

To another friend, speaking of her failing health, she says:

" I have always been so well that it requires a strong will-power and a great amount of grace to be submissive, but God is showing me that ' he directs my steps.' I have learned and accepted that ' he doeth all things well,' and now I believe from my inmost soul I can say, ' Thy will be done.'

12

For a time I *did* murmur; but a change has come
o'er the spirit of my dreams, and now "I have set
the Lord always before me; because he is at my
right hand I shall not be moved;" and why should
I murmur? He will "show me the path of life,"
and "in his presence is fullness of joy, at his right
hand are pleasures for evermore."

"*November* 12.

"MY DEAR ANNIE: Since coming to the city I
feel much better and stronger. I hope that I may
get well, and that God will favor the means used
for my recovery. But I am in the early stages of
consumption, and have a strong misgiving that
earth will not be my abiding place much longer.
Some days when I feel very weak, with hardly
strength to climb one pair of stairs, I am very low-
spirited; and the thought of leaving earth, and all
my loved ones, of relinquishing all my hopes for
future usefulness, drives me almost crazy, and my
heart has rebelled against my just and righteous
Father. Recently the Lord has led me to see that
'He doeth all things well,' and now I can say and
feel 'his will be done.' Being sick so much this
last year has unnerved me, so that it seems as if the·
least thing irritates me. O, Annie, great patience
should be used with those who are usually unwell.

I never thought it would weaken one's self-control
so much. If the Lord will let me live how I will
work for. him; but if otherwise ordained, how
happy I shall be to sit in the fullness of joy at his
right hand."

"*December* 27.

"The Christmas gift which pleased me most was
a picture of 'Faith standing before the Cross.' A
holy influence seems to steal over me while gazing
at it; that holy blood-stained cross where we may
come and have our sins removed. Last Sunday I
heard a sermon by Dr. M'Clintock on 'Forgive us
our trespasses, as we forgive those who trespass
against us.' In recounting our sins he said that
many faults which we tried to excuse as attribut-
able to weakness, habit, or circumstances, in the
eye of a pure and holy God would still be positive
sin; and that view of it came home to me, for
since my illness has so affected my whole body, I
find there has been a change in my moral nature.
Self-control I can hardly exercise, and too frequently I give way to irritability. I have tried to
excuse it on the ground of weakness; but that sermon, with God's blessing, has opened my eyes, so
I will pray for that grace which is sufficient for *all
things*."

On first coming to the city Mary had been anxious that we should review our former metaphysical studies, and we accordingly began with "Cousin's Elements of Psychology," alternately visiting each other's house for this purpose. The weather, however, soon became too severe and Mary too feeble to continue with any regularity the course we wished, and she was obliged to change her plans. At the invitation of our former teacher, Dr. V. N., we attended a course of lectures at his school, and Mary took much delight in thus, as it were, renewing her school-days. My hastening to the house to find her carefully and slowly dressing for our walk; the walk itself up Madison Avenue, both of us so happy, yet my joy mixed with sadness as I marked daily increasing feebleness; the pause in the lobby to allow her to cough and recover her breath; her eager entrance into our well-remembered study-hall, and the kindly greeting given to all she knew—how vividly do these things now come back to me! and her expectant face upturned to the lecturer, drinking in every word, and ever and anon by an inclination of the head, an appreciative glance to the friend at her side, or a pressure of the hand at some striking thought or suggestive passage. I remember once that Dr. Dwight, whose theme that day was "Earnestness," spoke particularly of the frivolous manner in which many young ladies spent their time, when their school-days were over, in adorning their persons and cultivating accomplishments only, instead of striving to be true Christian women. This lecture made a deep impression on Mary, who seemed unusually thoughtful on our way home. I said, "Dear, what did you think of the manner in which the doctor treated his subject to-day?" She answered so simply, "I am glad I did not do my hair in double rolls this morning." Dear child! so ready to make a personal application of every lesson. Would that more were as earnest in their life-work as yourself.

Mary was very industrious through all her illness, and particularly so at this time, taking much delight in plain sewing as well as fancy work; and the slippers which she worked for her brothers' Christmas gifts, the knitted shawls for her mother and others, as well as the numerous presents she made for her friends, will long be cherished as the last work of those busy fingers, now so still and cold.

Her mention of her brother's gift, "Faith at the Cross," recalls to my mind an incident related by her mother. She had brought from New Orleans a cross made of natural flowers, the work of a friend there; and shortly after New Year's, a young lady boarding in the same house gave Mary a raised cross constructed in a most beautiful manner. One day, after an unusual paroxysm of coughing, on lifting her head her glance rested on the two crosses on the mantle, and then turning to gaze on her brother's gift, with an expressive gesture she said, "Ma, three crosses, but where is the crown?" O, loved one, thou didst not know how soon that crown of righteousness, already laid up for thee by thy Lord himself, would be placed upon thy brow!

In the early part of February a change was deemed necessary, and Mary journeyed to the home of an uncle in Passaic. From this pleasant retreat, here are two letters:

"PASSAIC, *February* 18, 1865.

"MY DEAR FRIEND: The place from which this is written may surprise you, but I am spending a little time with my uncle, Dr. H., both my parents and himself thinking a change of air would be beneficial. This village is a quaint old place, settled more than a hundred years ago by Dutch farmers. In driving in this vicinity we have seen some ancieut stone farm-houses, and there is one which bears date 1715. My uncle has lived here more than ten years, and has a large country mansion. His family is of the same size as our own—eight children. It seems home-like to be here, for there are so many boy cousins, about the same age as my own dear brothers. They are all so kind to me that I am in a fair way to be spoiled. Why it is my fortune to have so many kind and loving friends, I do not understand. If my friends knew the wickedness and willfulness of my heart and life, they would, I fear, seek a worthier object. But weak and sinful as I am, I can truly say that I try to be sincere in all I do. I am very comfortable at present, and have great hopes of getting quite well. The coming months of March, April, and May, will be the most trying to one with my trouble, and if I can pass safely through them I may quite recover. I know that you will give me your prayers that the good Lord would grant this great desire of my heart.

"You ask what I have read this winter: I have been exceedingly interested in the 'Schonberg-Cotta' series. We have all the five. I agree with you that the 'Chronicles' are decidedly the best, though all are very interesting."

" Passaic, *February* 14.

"Dear Louise: They are all so kind and loving to me here, that sometimes a sense of great unworthiness comes over me when I receive any new mark of affection. . . . .

"I must assure you of an improvement in health, appetite, and spirits; and praying our Father in heaven to bless you abundantly,

"I am your own loving   "Mary."

On her return from P. a pleasant tour was projected by her parents to Maryland, *via* Baltimore and Washington, in hope that a sojourn iu a milder climate during our inclement spring season would aid the efforts to prolong the life of their much-loved child. The last afternoon before she left the city it was my privilege to spend with her; and though her affectionate farewell almost overcame me, I could not think that when next we met all that would be left would be but the shadow of my beautiful Mary.

The last letter received by me from Maryland is inserted almost entire:

" Westminster, *March* 21.

" Have you expected a letter from me ere this, my dear Louise? How many times have I felt the impulse to sit down and write to you, but oppor-

tunity or strength was wanting; so you have been
neglected until now. Our journey thus far has
been very pleasant. New scenes always possess a
charm for me, and then the companionship of my
dear parents has been delightful. In one week we
did up Philadelphia, Baltimore, and Washington
" brown," as pa would say. In the cars there was
a great deal to amuse us. You know any one pos-
sessing a funny streak can find endless amusement
in a car full of characters. . . . I think Baltimore
the nicest city we visited. It is much larger than
I had supposed, and very picturesquely situated on
several hills. On the top of one is the celebrated
Washington Monument, built of white marble. In
the streets around the monument are princely resi-
dences. . . . The city altogether is one of the most
beautiful I ever saw. I must not forget to tell
you that the streets are very clean. Washington
is the dirtiest city we were in, and you would not
wonder if you could see the immense trains of
army wagons continually passing through the
principal streets, and the number of military, both
cavalry and infantry, and such immense crowds of
strangers; it is either dust or mud all the time.
Our visit to the Capitol was very interesting; such
a magnificent dome towering up toward heaven,

and the great colonnades with double rows of immense marble columns! But the interior is much more beautiful. The ceilings are frescoed and gilded in the most elegant style, the floors inlaid in the rarest mosaics; the immense staircases are made of different kinds of marble; one of white marble was very beautiful. One piece of art excelled anything I ever saw, a pair of doors cast in bronze, and the principal scenes in the life of Columbus, from his birth to his death, depicted on them. They were cast in Europe.

"I bore the journey as well as could be expected, but was pretty well tired by the time I reached this place. However, now that I am nicely settled with my cousins, my health is beginning to revive. Yesterday Cousin John and I took a ride on horseback. We were gone an hour, and traveled the great distance of one mile and a half. Rather different from my former experiences with Romeo, is it not?

"Dear friend, still remember me in your prayers, and rest assured of my undiminished love. Do write often and keep me from getting homesick, for I shall miss ma so much when she leaves me. God ever bless you, dearest friend, is the prayer of your "MARY."

One little incident which occurred on the journey is brought to my mind just here. On her visit to the Capitol, of which she wrote to me with so much pleasure, after viewing the interior and coming down the front steps, she requested of her father that she might ascend on the other side and see the beautiful landscape of which she had heard so much. Her father tried to dissuade her from the attempt, fearing it would quite exhaust her, but she urged her wish till he consented.

Slowly and feebly, leaning on her father's arm, she at length gained the top, and turning to gaze on the lovely view, stood in rapt wonder and pleasure till the tears filled her eyes. Then moving closer to her mother's side, she softly said, "It will be something pleasant for me to remember by and by. Let us go now, pa." Did she think of the weary hours of pain and languishing which were just before her?

The story of her stay in Westminster has been written by an abler pen, that of Rev. John A. Munroe, the friend and relative with whom she sojourned there. He says:

"Being informed that a memorial of Cousin Mary is being prepared, I am happy to give some account of her latter days, as passed among us. That she came to us about the middle of March, and remained until within a week of her death, seems like a special act of favor toward us on the part of Providence : for she came to our home as comes a sweet melody ; she lingered as do the successive cadences of delightful music ; she departed as recede the gentle strains of harmony, whose echoes remain, a perpetual melody in our hearts.

"I recall her sojourn. How vivid! how like a present reality! Such features of her stay with us as seemed to reveal the progress or arrest of disease in her body, traced themselves deeply on the sympathies of my nature. I greatly rejoiced as she seemed to gather strength, after recovering from the fatigue of her journey from New York and Washington. After several weeks, even, she herself frequently spoke hopefully of a recovery, and talked much of a pleasant future. The opening of the spring seemed to awaken, for a brief time, these hopes. When she talked of the garden and flowers at home, she coupled with her desires and plans for them, desires and plans also for all the objects around, and inmates of, "Ashridge." This became especially noticeable and pleasant to me, because I based on it a hope that there was a change for the better in her physical condition. This is a feature of her life which I regret was lost to her parents and her home—this brief season, when she seemed to have wandered aside from that path leading *away* from earth, into a new path, full of the flowers of spring, gay with its birds and fresh with its atmosphere.

"It would have been a pleasure to you to see again, even as a passing vision, the buoyancy, the almost bounding life of Mary, reminding me of her days of health.

"She enjoyed greatly driving into the country. After two trials at horseback exercise, she yielded to my belief that it was too exhausting for her, and most cheerfully substituted carriage riding. On every bright day she expected one of these drives, anticipating them with much pleasure. During them she was unusually lively and communicative. Her enthusiasm over the scenery was charming and contagious. The blue hills in the distance suddenly sweeping into view, or the green wheat fields, nestling happily here and there, as if in favored spots, or some other feature among the rather meager ones of *early* spring, called forth impulsive expressions of delight.

"When thus moved by the influence of the scenery, she loved to converse on some of the many topics naturally suggested under such circumstances to a Christian mind, and generally showed a joyous recognition of the same God in nature as in her own heart. Her love of sacred poetry was, on one such occasion, well defined. We helped each other recall many beloved hymns. Among them were these: "From all that dwell below the skies;" "The spacious firmament on high;" "Before Jehovah's awful throne." One hymn she spoke of as especially pleasing in her communings with nature: "There seems a voice in every gale." She repeated it word by word, and it was beautifully appropriate, and feelingly recited.

"Even grace stands by in approving silence, unwilling to restrain the swelling of the heart and the falling of the tear, when we turn from this scene of life and promise to the change which follows, a harbinger of that scene or of those circumstances which made *Jesus weep*. While we knew it not, the destroyer was preparing for a sad, a fatal blow.

"Suddenly, unexpectedly, there comes first a check, then a loss of strength. We regretted the check; soon we mourned the little loss of strength; ere long we feared a decline. Each day suggested new hope against hope, only to disappoint; succeeding days increased our fears, and made the aching of the heart more painful. We wrote to her parents once, twice, thrice, but could not say, 'Come,' for it seemed like saying some sadder word.

"Meanwhile Mary was calm, resigned, and cheerful, only she grew somewhat weaker each two or three days. At first the pleasant drives must be postponed, the little walks omitted; the 'good-mornings' were given in bed, instead of coming from Cousin Mary toileted and ready to walk down to breakfast, as had been her custom. Her seat at the dinner-table next became sometimes vacant, and the cordial welcome she gave me when school labors were over must now be received up stairs.

"Her decline was comparatively gradual until within two days of her parents' arrival. During those days and the three following before she left us, terribly rapid was the change in feature, cough, and strength.

"Her suffering was extreme, her nerves hourly becoming weaker; slight exertion brought on spasms of torture in her spine. These spasms frequently broke her rest at night. On Friday, the day her mother and father came for her, the change seemed so marked that it was as if she had, while we gazed at her, suddenly placed one foot in the grave, and then lingered a few days in the consciousness of her position. We parted with her on Monday with the conviction that her life was ebbing away by the hour, though our hearts failed us to express that conviction to her parents, God having happily relieved us of a burden, in the assurance that his tender love and indulgence would permit her to live to bid adieu to brothers, sisters, and home. Not until two weeks before the time of her departure did I ever cease to hope for Mary's partial if not complete recovery. After that I treasured up every word, act, and look, as of one soon to join the angels.

" The social features of Mary's sojourn are also very visibly impressed upon my memory. Though no one could receive the impression that she was by nature a great talker, all felt free to seek the pleasures of her conversation.

" She was a minute observer and an intense sympathizer. All the family amusements and entertainments were exceedingly interesting to her.

Her imagination was frequently surprising, and there was almost a childish simplicity in her love of innocent amusement and fun. Once she was wearied from participating in the entertainments of the evening, and was reclining on the sofa, when she heard great merriment in an adjoining apartment. I remember the twinkle in her eye and the quiet laugh as she stood in the doorway for some time looking at the laughing group, not having been able to resist the impulse which prompted her to leave the embracing sofa and walk across the hall, that she might see as well as hear those merry ones.

"She would sit quietly and observe one member of the family, who was a famous tease, amuse himself in his peculiar way, and then suddenly and with great animation she would go to the assistance of the weaker party. Many times has she amused us by her earnest efforts at assisting thus. On these occasions there was a commingling of dignity and fun, of goodness and mirthfulness, such as can seldom be seen.

"The attentions Mary received did not lose their value in her estimation because she became an object of attention, and unable to help herself. From the young ladies of my school she received many bouquets and collections of mosses and grasses, which gave her great pleasure, and called forth expressions of gratitude. Mingled with all her intercourse there was a refinement of feeling and a spirit of purity always and keenly felt.

"She lost no opportunity of enforcing moral and religious truth; but her checks and reproofs were given in such a manner that none could ever wish they had not been received, though regretting the occasion for them.

"I found her on one occasion, with a company of young ladies around her, trying to impress upon them some important religious duty. The members of my class-meeting found great pleasure in coming to the house, on one occasion, that she might meet with us. The perfect resignation, trust, and peace indicated in her remarks affected several to tears.

"In thought and communion I think Mary lived much in heaven. She was alone a good deal, and in quiet, during our school hours, and none may know the sacredness of some of those seasons. When I bought for Sabbath-school use some little Testaments, handsomely bound, and fastened with clasps, she desired one of them, remarking that she wanted to have one in her pocket, and always with her.

"A prominent feature of her days here was her industry. She was never idle when feeling at all able to be profitably engaged. When not engaged in entertaining her friends or in reading, I always expected to find her sewing, or occupied with 'fancy needlework.'

"Another feature was her energy. She would not allow another to do for her what she could do for herself, unless from motives of gratifying one who desired to serve her. She performed every act of a complete toilet as long as strength remained, and except for the last few days of her visit here insisted on coming to the table to partake regularly of her meals, though she was at times compelled to be excused from her chair that she might recline upon the sofa. Her persistent letter-writing was a source of uneasiness to us; but it was useless to object unless we ourselves took her place as correspondent. She was devotedly attached to several friends, with whom, as well as with you and the children, she continued until the last a prompt and regular correspondence.

"To me there was a peculiar and always present attractiveness about dear Mary from the moment she entered our home until I gave her my last farewell. I would often forget the little life-burdens, and have its little heart-chills melted down in conversation with her. The beautiful in thought and the purifying in feeling, the joyousness of hope and the peacefulness of faith, often came to me in our intercourse.

"I was accustomed to ask while Mary was with us, and I often ask now, what was this peculiar attractiveness drawing all to Mary? Was it sympathy for her, as the sensitive heart would give sympathy to the beautiful unfolding rose suddenly blasted and withering? or was it the charm of heaven already insinuating itself in her being, giving that soft spiritual power to her countenance, and imparting to her presence something of the silent, exalting influence of the higher life? We thought not that so soon she would leave us all; yet sometimes I felt that she was being prepared either for a holier life here, or for a life which is altogether holiness.

"We hang her image in our hearts and embalm her two months' life with us in our memories. We are so selfish as to thank God that he gave us so many of her latter days, days of development for heaven.

"We use her presence in the spirit-world as a means of bringing heaven very near to us, for our late communication with her was not destroyed, but only modified by her bodily departure from us, and it seems that her freed spirit is now nearer us than when it was shut up in the wasting form that held it.

"Beloved friend! angel Mary! we will not so much mourn for you as we will cultivate an acquaintance with you in your new sphere. We think of your happy departure, and rising with you on the wings of your triumph, we call you thrice blessed, for the bedside glimpses of glory were but the faintest dawnings of the day of heaven that then commenced breaking to your vision; the clouds of mortality being swept away you 'see Him as he is,' and you 'know even as you are known.'"

Even as the tear falls over this charming tribute to our dear one's worth, we must turn back a little in our narrative, and read her own story of her stay with her cousins. We linger long over these few letters, for they are the last which her feeble hand had strength to write, and we feel that to us they have untold value.

"The other day I was sitting in an easy-chair, feeling very sick and dispirited, and so weak that I could scarcely get dressed, when pa came in and handed me your letter. After perusing it I felt much comforted, and could say from my heart, 'Though He slay me yet will I trust in him.' How sweet is Christian sympathy! I cling to your love so much now that I am an invalid. Friends are so kind and thoughtful here.

"The weather has been perfectly lovely for several days, and it is wonderful what a change it makes in my feelings. Yesterday C. and I took a nice little ride to a hill not far distant, where there is a lovely prospect, and off in the horizon the outlines of the 'Blue Ridge' are clearly seen. It seemed strange that C. and I should be riding over the hills of Maryland; but I have ceased to wonder at changes. Somehow, Aunt Etta, the conviction grows stronger with me every day, that the seal has been set upon my forehead, and I am numbered among those who will soon be in glory. I rejoice at the prospect of a speedy release; but my constant prayer is, 'Lord, teach me not only to do but to suffer thy will.' And I would that affliction and weakness be continued if I may only be perfect.

The Saviour does comfort me, and uphold my drooping spirit with his loving arm. Continue to pray much for your loving "MARY."

"April 1.

"DEAR COUSIN ANNIE: My health is very miserable; for three months my strength has failed very fast, until now I am but a shadow of my former self. I do not suffer much pain, though occasionally very severe attacks of pain in the left lung, or just below it, seize me, and render me very ill. But this racking cough is wearing my life away, and there is a general sinking of the whole system. In May I expect to go to Minnesota to spend some months; that is, if I live, and I am so afraid I shall miss seeing you when you come East. C. is spending a part of his vacation with me, and how we enjoy each other's society! We were sitting in the parlor this morning in company with a young lady, and suddenly she asked, 'Where will we all be this time next year?' and like a flash it came to me, '*your* resting-place will be in heaven.' And Annie, dear, I long to depart and be with Christ; 'for me to die is gain.' My life has been full of the richest blessings, and I had hoped that God would permit me to live and labor for him.

But he chooses rather that I should suffer affliction
and thus glorify his holy name.   And I thank him
that he keeps me generally cheerful and patient.

"Yours ever,   "MARY."

"*April* 6.

"DEAR FATHER: I feel like congratulating you
all that the debt of Thirtieth-street is paid.   Last
Sabbath must indeed have been a day of rejoicing,
and I am glad that the Church is free.   May the gospel clarion ever ring out in clear tones, 'Ho, every
one that thirsteth, come ye to the waters; and he
that hath no money, come ye, buy and eat; yea,
come, buy wine and milk without money and without price.'   Thirtieth-street has been the birthplace
of many souls, and God grant that a countless number may yet become the children of the kingdom
through its influence.   Have I not reason to remember its altars, where nine years ago the Holy Spirit
strove with me, and in accents sweet taught me to
feel that Christ was waiting for me?   And I gave
myself to him; but not entirely.   Else why this
severe probation through which he is leading me?
He saw, when I fondly hoped that my whole heart
was his, that there was something lacking, and he
found it necessary to crush all earthly hopes by

passing me through the furnace of affliction
Now I humbly believe that he has full possession
of my heart, and I have no other desire than to act
his perfect will."

"*April* 25.

"I do long for home so much, but it is no use to
be impatient; and I feel contented most of the
time. The Lord is with me, and I am happy in his
love. Dear Louise, I cannot write much longer,
I am so tired. Give my love to all. I am your
loving "MARY."

"*April* 29.

"It is hard to do and suffer the Lord's will in
everything; but he has led me through deep waters,
and his hand sustains me. 'Though he slay me,
yet will I trust in him.'"

CHAPTER IX.*

" THE LAST OF EARTH."

" ' Sleep soft, beloved ! ' we sometimes say,
But have no tune to charm away   .
Sad dreams that through the eyelids creep.
But never doleful dream again,
Shall break the happy siumber, when
He giveth his beloved sleep."

WHEN Mary's parents, bidding her adieu, left her
to the care of their kind relatives in Maryland,
it was agreed that if she began to fail they were to
be sent for. On Wednesday, May 3, they received
the dispatch requesting them to come, and by Friday noon they were at her side. On entering her
chamber the whole truth was revealed ; could this
be indeed their Mary? Their hearts were filled
with sorrow, and hope at once fled. That sunken
face would never again resume its wonted beauty,
that emaciated body never regain its rounded
form; nothing was left but to minister to her comfort, and soothe her short journey to the brink of the

---

* Most of the particulars contained in this chapter were fur-
nished by Mary's father.

river. But they *could not* see her die away from
home; while strength lasted they must haste.
Watching with intense interest all that day and
weary night, they tried to alleviate her suffering
and cool her fevered brow. Racked with incessant
coughing spells throughout Friday night, the morning found her faint and wearied, yet cheerful and
serene. About nine o'clock her father prayed, sang,
and conversed with her, apparently much to her
comfort. She requested that the reading should be
from the Gospels, remarking that lately she took
especial pleasure in that portion of the Scripture.
The hymn sung was of her own choice :

> " There is an hour of peaceful rest,
> To mourning wanderers given."

The conversation was very interesting, her mind
being so tranquil, and she seemed so submissive to
the will of her heavenly Father.

During Saturday and the following night she
was in much pain and weakness, from continued
fever and distressing cough, and could only talk in
short sentences ; but on Sunday morning she was
rather relieved, and as early as eight o'clock was
ready to have her father read and converse with
her. He selected 1 Corinthians xv, Paul's grand

argument on the resurrection, to which she listened
with fixed attention, and asked him to pause more
than once while she analyzed the meaning of several passages.

So severe had been her sufferings during the
previous night that she called her father's attention
to a passage in Psalm cxxx, "More than they
that watch for the morning,' and said, 'Dear pa,
I know what that means; how have I watched
for the morning!"

On Monday morning she was dressed for the
journey, and many prayers went up from anxious
hearts that the Lord would support her till she
reached her much-loved home. When prepared
to start, with the fortitude and resolution that had
always marked her character, she walked from the
room, and putting her hand on the balustrade,
would have descended the stairs without assistance, but found it necessary to lean on her father's arm. Attended by the dear friends from
Westminster, they were soon seated in the cars
and on their way to Baltimore, which they reached
at one in the afternoon. On Tuesday morning the
cars were taken for Philadelphia, where they
arrived late in the afternoon; but on asking Mary
if she would stop here, she declined, her only

thought being 'home, home.' They accordingly hastened on, reaching Jersey City about sunset. Another night of suffering. O patient child, 'a little while' and you 'shall enter into rest.'

In the morning the last stage of the journey was begun, and while waiting their arrival in the railroad station, I saw them support my dear friend to the car. What a fearful change had those nine weeks made! The look of suffering on her face was only less noticeable than the weary droop of the beautiful head, and the patient folding of the thin hands, and the lusterless eye seemed as if looking at " Him who is invisible." How she welcomed me, saying in a slow whisper, " Come and see me soon, soon; I have so much to say to you." I rejoiced to aid in comfortably seating her in the cars for the last two hours' ride, and stooping to kiss her, she said, "I want to get home—sweet home." That was my last sight of my friend.

Other friends met the mournful party in the cars, and many a silent tear was dropped as they looked upon the dear invalid and memory recalled the beautiful vision of perfect health they had been wont to call Mary. On reaching Ashridge her father carried her into the sitting-room, where she greeted all the family, and afterward in those same loving arms was borne to her own lovely room. Of the fatigue consequent upon the hasty traveling it avails not now to speak; it seemed almost forgotten by Mary in her joy at being once more under her father's roof. Through Wednesday night and Thursday she suffered much, yet would insist on sitting in her easy chair and working on her embroidery.

On Thursday night, while her nurse was at her bedside, Mary said to her, "Fanny, do you know the hymn called 'Wrestling Jacob?'"

"Yes, I do," was Fanny's reply.

"Well," said Mary, "this is it," pointing to herself; "this represents wrestling till the break of day; no poetry can describe this," meaning her agony.

Fanny then asked her how she felt; she answered, "Peaceful," and presently sunk into a doze.

On Friday morning she was tranquil, and sat up several hours, working a part of the time on a pair of slippers intended for a favorite uncle. While sitting in her easy chair she remarked to her mother, "Ma, if I feel as well on Sunday as I do now, I shall be able to go down stairs." In the afternoon, however, her sufferings were renewed, and continued with intensity during the long night.

This was the period of her sharpest agony, and her parents were so engaged in trying to relieve her that very little conversation took place; indeed, they began to join her in prayer that her sufferings might be shortened.

In the middle of the night, while in much bodily distress, she said to her nurse, "Fanny, I have just been wondering what I have done that I should suffer so." The nurse replied, "You know, dear, 'whom the Lord loveth he chasteneth.'" "O yes," she answered, and presently dropped asleep.

It was on the previous evening that the physician had visited her, and she asked him to tell her candidly what he thought of her situation; but he evaded a direct answer. After he left, she said, "The doctor is like every body else, he has no hope." The nurse replied, "You know nothing is impossible with God; what did the doctor say?" "I asked him if there was any hope of my getting well, and he said, 'We'll see,' and said I could eat what I wished;" and putting on a smile, she continued, " *This* is impossible," meaning her recovery.

On Saturday morning about six o'clock she fell into a quiet sleep, the first of any length she had enjoyed since noon of the day before. On waking, her mother read to her the ninetieth psalm, which was always a favorite of Mary's. Her cough had left her on Friday, so that now she suffered chiefly from weakness and shortness of breath.

During the morning, while her grandmother was sitting beside her, Mary remarked, "I may struggle along through the summer, but I shall drop away in the fall; I feel I have a great work to do." Her grandmother said, "What work, Mary?"

She replied, "To prepare my soul to enter into the heavenly rest."

About the middle of the morning she was placed in the easy chair, at her own request, saying to her mother, "I wish to sit up just two hours;" then looking at the clock, "What shall I do these two hours? I can't be idle."

Her embroidery was brought, and she worked on it a few minutes at a time, till so exhausted it was taken from her hands. Before being placed in the chair she said to her mother, "Am I impatient? I try not to be."

She adhered to her purpose of sitting up for two hours, and at the end of that time requested to lie down, and feeling very weak, she said, "I am just like a babe."

During the afternoon a kind young neighbor brought a beautiful bouquet of rare flowers, which afforded much pleasure, particularly the "lilies of the valley," which she quickly discovered and pointed out, remarking upon their beauty and fragrance. Late in the afternoon she desired to sit in her chair by the window, that she might look upon the lovely landscape bathed in the glory of the setting sun. It was but a momentary enjoyment, for she was seized with sudden weakness and shortness of breath which turned all attention to herself. After family prayers, which were held in her room, arrangements were made for the night, and she seemed more comfortable, but hourly growing weaker.

Soon after midnight, her parents having retired for a short rest, and her favorite nurse watching beside her, the following conversation took place:

"Fanny, do you think I have failed much since I came home?"

"Yes," replied Fanny, "I think you have."

"Do you think I have been impatient?"

"Why no, indeed. I think you bear your sufferings very well."

"There is one unfavorable symptom, Fanny, for I heard ma and Aunt Jane talking about it when

14

they thought I was asleep. My cough has left me. Do *you* really think I am worse?"

"Yes, dear, I do think you are very much worse; but how do you feel about yourself? how do you feel in your mind?"

Mary put out her hands and answered, "I feel perfectly happy, and if I die before morning, I know the Lord will take me home." And looking earnestly at Fanny, she added, "I hope I put on no vainglory, but I am loosed from every shackle of earth."

She presently said, "This is Saturday night."

Looking at the clock, Fanny replied, "We may call it Sunday morning."

Mary continued, "If I am spared through the day, I will call all the family together to have a little talk with them."

Then followed a conversation about distributing her "trinkets," as she called her little treasures. Afterward she said, "This is Sunday, and on Monday night Louise will come up, and then I want to have a good long time with her alone."

Presently her Aunt Jane came to her bedside, and Mary asked her to read; and when her aunt asked, "What shall I read?" Mary answered, "Some gospel truths."

After that she slept quietly till five in the morning, when, as she seemed sinking rapidly, the family were called in.

Her mother, wishing to see if she was conscious of her condition, leaned over her and said, "Daughter, do you remember the beautiful text Louisa sent you, 'He giveth his beloved sleep?'"

She replied, "Who is dead now?" evidently not comprehending the remark.

Her mother answered, "Nobody, but if it is the Lord's will to take you very soon, do you feel that 'He giveth his beloved sleep?'"

Mary replied with emphasis, "Certainly, ma."

She was now very weak and short of breath, and evidently understanding by the words and looks of all about her that they thought her death was near, she said to her mother "Ma, do you think I shall die *to-day?*"

"I do not know, dear, but I think you will."

"This is unexpected," she said, manifesting surprise. "I thought I should linger several months."

Her mother responded, "Well, dear, if the Lord should see fit to cut short your sufferings, you would be willing?"

"O yes," was her ready answer; "but I would be willing to endure suffering for the sake of being with you all a little longer, I have been away from home so much lately. I want Mr. Foss to come and pray with me."

But Mr. Foss was far away; and though Mary, forgetting this in her hour of extremity, yearned for the presence of the pastor who had received her into the Church so long ago, it was impossible to send him word.

Presently she was heard to say in a whisper, clasping her hands, "The Lord is my shepherd." She now began to dispose of her personal treasures, but had only mentioned a few, when she became too exhausted to proceed.

Her mother then said, "What shall I tell Charlie for you?" referring to her brother at college.

"Give him my warmest love; he knows what I am; tell him to meet me in heaven."

Soon after she asked her father to read the twelfth of Hebrews, to which she listened with attention. When he reached the verse, "But ye are come unto Mount Zion," she was specially interested; and when reading the passage, "and to Jesus the Mediator," her face was lighted with an angelic smile. At her request was sung "Rock of Ages," and during the singing she repeated with her lips every word.

It was then suggested that the hymn be read, "How happy every child of grace," which was always a great favorite of Mary's. Her father took up the Church hymn book to read from, but she shook her head and said, "No, no, the other book," referring to a volume of Charles Wesley's sacred poetry, which had been her daily companion during her absence in Maryland. While her father read verse after verse, she was fixed in her attention, and drank in every word. Coming to the passage,

> "What is there here to court my stay,
> Or keep me back from home,"

she quickly and clearly repeated the remaining couplet:

> "While angels beckon me away,
> And Jesus bids me come?"

After finishing the poem, her father stepped into another room, but was quickly called back, as Mary wished him to pray. All knelt during prayer, and none seemed more interested than the dear object of the petitions.

After this, while her mother was leaning over her, she said, "You have been a good mother to me;" and inclining her head toward her father, she added, "and father too."

In a few moments she was heard to say, "Why don't he come?"

The nurse said, "Who?"

"Jesus; I want to die."

Presently she seemed distressed, and said, "I wish I could die right away."

Turning to her faithful nurse and grasping her hand, she said very earnestly,

"Fanny, I love you; in this world I can never repay you, but the Lord will reward you. Meet me in heaven."

In a moment she inquired, "Fanny, am I worse?"

"Yes, dear, you are sinking very fast."

"Where's ma? call her."

Her mother, who had stepped into an adjoining room to compose herself, returned and said, "Well, dear?" Mary said, "You will dispose of all my trinkets in a sensible manner."

Her mother now said, "What shall I tell Louisa for you?"

"O what a trial to go without seeing her! tell her to meet me in heaven."

"What shall I tell Florence?"

"I wanted to talk to Florence; tell *her* to meet me in heaven."

" What shall I say to Miss Lindsay ? "

Making a significant motion with her head, she answered, "How I love her! Tell her to meet me in heaven."

" Have you any message for Cousin Annie ? "

"I have *written* to her."

" What shall I tell Cousin John and Fanny ? "

" Tell them I love them, to meet me in heaven, and to do all the good they can while here below."

After sending her love to an absent uncle, and requesting that the slippers she was working for him might be given him, she uttered such expressions as these: " Jesus, take me ; " " I am going, going." Her sight began to fail, when she said, "How queer! I see it—white." Again she uttered, "How queer! I can't see—more light."

The shutters were now thrown wide open, when she said, " It don't last."

Her aunt now asked her, " Can you see Aunt Janie ? "

She replied, " I can see a little."

Her mother kissed her forehead, when Mary whispered, " I want to kiss them all."

Her father held up the little children one by one, whom she kissed, and said " Good-night " to each ; mentioning the name of only one, the young-

est, to whom she said " Good-night, Allie." And
now as they all stood round the dying saint, she
spread her hands and said :

" Good-night, good-night; our Father in heaven
will take care of you all."

Her father said to her, " Daughter, is the way
still clear ? "

" Yes," she replied, " very, *very* clear."

This was her last response, and was it not fitting
to be her last ?   The brightness of her path was
growing into " perfect day," and should she not
say " Very, *very* clear ? "

Presently she was heard to whisper, " Why am I
taken and the others left ?   Then she exclaimed,
" Home, home, sweet home ; heaven is my home,"
and then every breath was " home," until the last
faint word seemed echoed from the heavenly shore,
and we knew that our loved one had " entered
into rest."

And so on that holy Sabbath our Mary passed
away in the lovely freshness of the spring morning, with the birds singing sweetly, the sun shining
brightly, the breezes playing softly, passed away
from the beauties of earth to the glories of heaven.

Her peaceful death was a fitting end to her earnest and useful life.

To us is left her empty chair, her vacant chamber, and her hallowed grave, with the priceless memories of her beautiful, holy life.

> "We miss her in the place of prayer,
>   And by the hearth-fires bright:
> We pause beside her door to hear
>   Once more her sweet good-night."

We mourn our loss, but to *her* "to die was gain."

On the day after Mary died a little company of friends came to pay the last tribute of respect to those precious remains, and through those rooms of which she had so often been the graceful ornament softly rang these fitting lines:

> "How blest the righteous when he dies!
>   When sinks a weary soul to rest,
> How mildly beam the closing eyes!
>   How gently heaves th' expiring breast!

> "Farewell, conflicting hopes and fears,
>   Where lights and shades alternate dwell:
> How bright th' unchanging morn appears!
>   Farewell, inconstant world, farewell!"

And on Tuesday morning they bore our loved one to the church of her youth, and laid her within that altar where she first consecrated herself to the Lord. In an open coffin, with her hands clasped over a cross of flowers, and a crown of lovely blossoms at her head, lay "the beautiful clay," which was all that was left to us. The house was crowded with friends who met to mourn their loss; but their mourning was turned to joy at hearing how the Lord had supported her in her last hours, and ministered to her an "abundant entrance" into the kingdom.

Said one, in speaking of the impressive occasion, "It seemed more like a time of joy than sadness, for each heart was gladdened at hearing of her triumphant death, and all united in thanking her Master for her useful life."

And when at sunset we stood around her open grave on the green slope of a lovely hill in Greenwood, "we thought how we had sighed that she might find an atmosphere, in Minnesota or elsewhere, so balmy as to heal her wounded lungs, and give her health, and ease, and vigor. She *has* found it, all perfumed with immortality, near the throne. All to her is gain: health for sickness; life for death; the associations of heaven for those of earth; the full expansion and development of eternity for the slowly opening energies of time; the crown of glory for the cross of suffering.

"O friend! O sister! not in vain
Thy life, so calm and true ;
The silver dropping of the rain ;
The fall of summer dew !

"How many burdened hearts have prayed
　Their lives like thine might be!
But more shall pray henceforth for aid
　To lay them down like thee."

"By the bright waters now thy lot is cast,
Joy for thee, happy friend! thy bark hath past
　　The rough sea's foam!

"Now the long yearnings of thy soul are stilled,
Home, home! thy peace is won, thy heart is filled:
　　Thou art gone home!"
　　　　　　　　　　　HEMANS.

As I have prosecuted this loving task, I have
found myself, many times, pondering this question:
What was that which constituted the peculiar
power and charm of Mary's life? As I view it, it
consisted of many blended beauties, of which, more
prominent than the rest, were that look and manner our Saviour must have had when he said,
"Wist ye not I must be about my father's business;" that strange earnestness of expression
which marked a soul intent upon some noble, lofty
purpose; that conscientiousness so delicate, so sensitive, taking alarm at every intimation of wrong,
and keeping the soul forever on its guard; that
transparent purity and simplicity, even of the imagination, before which indelicacy stood abashed; that
lovingness of heart, ever overflowing in beneficent
activities, in thoughts and words and deeds of love,

in holy ministries of affection toward all with whom a gracious Providence temporarily associated her.

And now my loving task is done. It has been a joy to rehearse the story of my friend's life, and I have tried to tell it as it was, in its every-day incidents, in its trials and crosses, as well as its joys and pleasures; and if in the heart of any reader there has been awakened one earnest desire to be more devoted to the service of our blessed Master, and more helpful to our fellow-pilgrims in the way to heaven, "Not unto us, O Lord, not unto us, but unto thy name be glory."

MARY'S BROTHER.

The Sister's Call.

A voice from the spirit-land,
  A voice from the silent tomb,
Entreats with a sweet command,
      Brother, come home!

List, list! 'tis a sister gone;
  Unseen, yet where'er I roam,
She calls from her star-lit throne,
      Brother, come home!

At eve, when the crimson west
  Is dyed by the setting sun,
She calls like a spirit blest,
      Brother, come home!

Abroad in the stilly night,
  A stranger and all alone,
I hear through the misty light,
      Brother, come home!

In dreams of the midnight.deep,
  When angels of mercy come,
I startle to hear in sleep,
      Brother, come home!

When far from my father's hearth,
  I sail o'er the white sea foam,
I hear through the storm wind's mirth,
      Brother, come home!

By sorrow and sin oppressed,
  She answers to every moan,
"Come here, where the weary rest,"
      Brother, come home!

Ah, loved one, I haste to thee;
  Soon, soon shall I reach thy home;
And there wilt thou welcome me,
      I come! I come!

MARY'S BROTHER.

G. ADOLPHUS NORTH

DIED AT SEA, MAY 16, 1866, AGED 17 YEARS AND
10 MONTHS.

WHEN I took my pen, not three months ago, to
leave a simple record of my dear Mary's life, I had
no thought of this supplementary chapter; but
when interrupted in my labor by the summons to
that lovely hill, once more sanctified by a believer's
death, I solicited and obtained the privilege of lay-
ing this tribute of love on Dolphie's grave.

Adolphus was our Mary's second brother, and
at the time she left us he was not seventeen years
old. Six years before, his mind had been in an
especial manner turned toward heavenly things,
and all who know him unite in saying he had tried
to be a Christian child.

And Dolph had much to struggle against; his
sister and brothers were all quieter and more serious children than he. When yet very young, he
showed a restlessness of manner and an inordinate

love of fun, which, with his inquiring mind and active body, often led him into mischief. His powers of mimicry were very great, and we cannot recollect without a smile the funny gestures and quaint ways with which, as a boy, he would amuse us. Anything odd or ludicrous at any place would seem irresistibly to affect him, and his parents often dreaded lest this propensity might overcome his more serious moments, and render fruitless their endeavors to give stability to his character.

But when he gave his heart to the Lord, though only eleven years of age, it was with a determination to fight manfully under his banner, not only against the world and the devil, but against self; and though often almost discouraged and overcome, he would not give up the struggle.

All the best and purest feelings of his nature had been gradually developed, till, during the winter that Mary spent in the South, when the eldest brother was in college, and the father away many weeks on business, we were all astonished to notice how much of a man Dolphie had become. He coveted earnestly the best gifts, and " whatsoever things are pure, whatsoever things are lovely, whatsoever things are of good report," he not only made the subject of his thoughts, but also of his prayers and efforts.

When Mary passed away her mantle seemed to fall on Dolph, and none was more obliging, more loving, more Christ-like than he. A letter written by him on his seventeenth birthday will show him as he was the last two years:

"Dear Mother: I can scarcely express my feelings on this seventeenth birthday, so many things crowd upon my thoughts. I look back upon my past life, and find, to my great grief, that it has fallen far short of the standard which I should have attained. And when I think of it, I am filled with amazement that my heavenly Father has in so great mercy preserved my days unto the present. It is my firm desire and determination, my dear mother, to follow hereafter more rigidly the footsteps of our blessed Saviour, that I may in all the various walks of life evince a disposition to what is right and well-pleasing in the sight of God. Will you and pa add your prayers that I may carry out my resolution, and thereby experience that 'peace which passeth understanding?' Especially this day I can look forward to the time when I must be something—must be a man, must occupy some position among men ; and O, may God's grace assist me in my efforts from henceforth to prepare myself for life's great struggle, that I may do honor both to my parents and my God.

"I feel, moreover, that, Charlie being away from home so much, and the position of eldest child at home falling upon me, I must be an example to my younger brothers and sisters, and with the assistance of our heavenly Father I mean that it shall be a good one. God help me! Dear mother, I feel that the death of dear sister has been, and will be, beneficial to me; and O, why should it not? Was there ever a more lovely and perfect example of true holiness? I pray God that a double portion of it may rest upon me. And now, above all, I need your prayers to sustain me in my resolutions. I know that I have been a forgetful, disobedient, and wayward child, grieving my parents much and oft, besides disregarding God's holy law; but I firmly hope that with divine aid I may redeem my character, and fully make up for what I have lost. This I ask for Jesus's sake.

"Your most affectionate son,   "DOLPH."

Shortly after this, on a pleasant day in August, there gathered in the cool sitting-room at "Ash-

ridge" a friendly party of six young folks. We
had often before met thus, but now our number
was broken—one was detained by other engage-
ments, and one "was not," for God had taken
her. The greetings were subdued, the merry
laugh was quieter, and the quick repartee was
checked; and when we heard a step on the stair,
or a door opened, we involuntarily waited to hear
Mary's welcome, and to see her loving face; but
she came not.

As we ascended the stairs, and turned toward
the familiar room, we almost expected, on entering, to meet her. Over the mantle hung her much-
prized "crosses;" at one side a picture of the
good ship "Winthrop;" (a birthday gift only a
year before;) and over the bed hung the cross and
crown of flowers taken from her coffin—all the
same; on the table her Bible, in one corner her
work-basket and sewing-chair—and she who gave
a charm to all was gone from our midst.

But her spirit hovered over us, and when we
gathered, a happy group, at our diversions or our
more serious employments, we could not, we would
not forget her. And even then we said aside
to each other, "How much Dolph is like Mary!
how good he is growing!" Dear boy, already

the light of heaven was on his brow and we knew it not.

On Sabbath afternoon we slowly walked to the little school-house, and from the lips of one of our number (almost a stranger yet a friend) we heard an earnest, loving exposition of those words of our Saviour : " Whosoever will come after me, let him deny himself, and take up his cross and follow me." How well I recall the hymn we sang so softly at the close of our service:

> " Must Jesus bear the cross alone,
>   And all the world go free?
> No, there's a cross for every one,
>   And there's a cross for me.
>
> " How happy are the saints above,
>   Who once went sorrowing here ;
> But now they taste unmingled love,
>   And joy without a tear."

I cannot help thinking that then and there, while remembering our saint above, and influenced by those earnest words addressed to all who would come after Christ and be his disciples, Dolph was strengthened in his birthday resolves, and determined that nothing should separate him " from the love of God."

Through all the summer he daily grew in favor with God and man ; and though a mother's loving ear heard a slight cough, and her watchful eye detected some signs of weariness at times, yet we thought Dolph is only growing; as soon as cool weather comes he will be stronger.

The cooler days drew on apace, and in September Dolph and his young brother began to go daily to the city to school. Already he had laid his plans for the improvement of his mind during the coming winter; already he had commenced, with the hope and anticipation of youth, to look forward to the close of this school year, when he would enter college while yet his brother remained there.

But as the October days grew chilly his cough became apparent to all; the healthful color left his cheeks; and with almost nervous haste, remembering Mary's decline, his parents first consulted the family physician, and then carried Dolph to an experienced lung doctor. Rest and a change of air were prescribed; if possible, a sea voyage. This intelligence fell like a shock on a large circle of friends, for, even while yet unconscious of his illness, disease had made fearful inroads on his frame.

Meanwhile our sympathies were more fully awakened for Dolph on account of our solicitude for the health of my own brother, whose physician had recommended the same remedy. From this

time how many plans were discussed, how many
ways proposed, for sending the two lads from
home!

Thus came to a hasty end all Dolph's pleasant
hopes for the future, and the whole current of his
thoughts was changed. During the anxious two
months which now elapsed, he went quietly in and
out at home, reading and resting, and on the few
fine days which autumn afforded, taking such exercise as his strength would permit. The prayers
of many were offered for his recovery, and many
were the kind inquiries and loving messages sent
by friends to the home on the hill.

His schoolmates, with whom he was thus suddenly called to part, will long cherish his pleasant
memory. An extract from a letter of his much
esteemed teacher will show us Dolph as a school-
boy:

" As my relations to Adolphus were such as.
necessarily to give me very close and very clear
views of his mental constitution, it may not, perhaps, be altogether out of place for me to point to
at least one trait by which he was remarkably distinguished. I mean his *docility*. He was docile
in that double sense, which consists in being both
able to be taught, and *willing* to be taught. Not

that he was endowed with any extraordinary powers of natural genius, though his capacity was decidedly good; but that his ready appreciative spirit always cordially seconded the efforts of his instructor. Under the influence of this spirit, difficulties failed to operate as discouragements; diligence showed itself in his preparations; and, in his recitations, when you paused to amplify or explain, there was a sustained attention which further showed that,·in things intellectual as in things moral and religious, he had learned obedience to the precept, 'Take heed what ye hear.'"

Counting this an admirable trait, I should be tempted strongly to press it for imitation. I should, indeed, make it the chief feature; for it gave, I doubt not, the principal charm to his whole character. This lovely docility inclined his ear, and kept it inclined to that best of all teachers, who said, "Learn of *me*."

This will account for the esteem in which he was held in the Bible class. This alone will duly account for the patient, nay, the cheerful submission with which he met the painful teachings of his last year.

Intent on the setting forth of a single point, because in that I see, or think I see, the main lesson of that brief though beautiful life, I pass over what some might think most important to be considered in this connection; such things, for example, as ordinary manners, etc. On this it is quite enough for me to say, that his bearing was a constant exhibition of the proprieties of Christian character.

In the early part of November it was decided to send our dear boys to South America, to the care of one of our missionaries at Buenos Ayres; and, as the Missionary Board were about sending another laborer to that part of the field, the opportunity was gladly embraced of sending our invalids in his company. After numerous delays the date of sailing was fixed at the twentieth, and preparations were hurriedly but carefully made for the two young travelers leaving home. Of the *last* Sabbath we cannot think but with peculiar emotions. That Dolph was very ill could no longer be doubted; his hollow cough, his sunken cheeks, his feeble step, were apparent to all; but through and above the traces of suffering we could see his hope and his resignation.

It had always been the custom with his parents to make every important event in the family circle of as much interest as possible to all its members; and no great step was ever taken without asking

the blessings of God upon the effort. On this Sabbath evening the family assembled in the pleasant
sitting-room for a prayer and experience meeting,
and after singing a hymn of praise, and committing
their loved one to the tender mercy of the Lord,
each in turn rose to tell of his hopes and fears, and
prayers for Dolph. And while one spoke of his
consistent example, another of his patience and
kindness, and a third of his efforts to lead others
to the Saviour, Dolph seemed much affected. After
all had spoken he said, " This is the first time I
ever thought I had done good to anybody." Then
he told of his love for his Redeemer, of his trust
in his merits, of his hope of recovery, and ended
by assuring his parents that he would "stand up
for Jesus."

The next day we met him at the ship, but
unexpected delays prevented it sailing at the
time appointed, so for two days the family waited
in the city, and on the third, early in the morning,
we said farewell to the young voyagers, not
knowing whether we should look on their faces
again.

The feelings of a father found vent in these lines,
which were Dolph's constant study during his
voyage:

TO MY DEAR DOLPH.

" Go forth, my son, the vessel's deck to tread,
    With firm, if not elastic step ;
Resolved to meet each storm and angry sea
    In God's great name, who guideth thee.

" In hours of feebleness, when longing thoughts
    Of loving ones, left far behind,
Steal o'er thy heart, and bring the tear and sigh,
    Forget not thou that God is nigh.

" Not in the storm alone will he appear,
    Soft saying to the winds, ' Be still : '
But closer yet, within thy troubled breast,
    The Saviour's voice shall give thee rest.

" ' Rest for the weary,' thou hast often sung ;
    Meaningless, in the lap of ease ;
But thou shalt know in perils of the deep,
    ' He giveth his beloved sleep.'

" So when on Argentina's shores thou'lt tread,
    Where other gods than thine are served,
And sin in garb of pleasure bids thee yield,
    Then cover thee with Christ, thy shield.

" I know thee, Dolph ; in sickness thou wilt prove
    How precious is the grace of Christ ;
Meekly bending, thou'lt kiss th' outstretch'd rod,
    In suffering still honoring God.

" Or if reviving health shall give thee strength,
    Thou'lt use that strength in sowing wide
The gospel seed, upon that barren soil,
    And so shalt bless those sons of toil.

" O son ! my dearly loved, thy unfill'd seat
    At table, or the place of prayer,
Shall morn and eve to th' pensive group recall
    Thy pleasant face, so dear to all.

"A favored father I, and highly blest
  With children of such precious worth:
Seven living; one is not, yet *is*—
  A joyous white-robed saint in bliss.

"Next her, because the chast'ning hand is laid,
  Thou dearest art of all the group;
And O, my boy, this parting's mixed with pain
  Lest we shall never meet again.

"No! never's not the word; we'll meet again.
  If not here, yet in th' other world
Where darling Mary's gone before to greet
  Father and son, who there shall meet."

When the pilot left the ship the boys sent by him their first letters for home. Dolphie's I insert:

"*Going down the Harbor*, 12¼ *o'clock, Dec.* 20, 1865.

"DEAR MOTHER: We find that we will have a chance to send home by the pilot. Pa can tell how we reached the vessel, and our parting. I watched the folks till they were out of sight, lost among the ships and docks. I have fussed around the cabin some, and have got things somewhat to rights, and have also been out to watch the sailors hoist sail, etc. Their voices, as they work, are very musical. Well, as to myself, I am very calm and hopeful, not desponding in the least. And now, dear mother, don't allow yourself to repine or be low-spirited on my account. I am in the Lord's hands, and am sure he will direct all things for our good. I don't want you to think of me as *poor* Dolph, but as *happy* Dolph—cheerful, and making the best of everything. Dear mother, how much I love you I never can tell; no one knows but our Father. O! can I ever repay the years of care and love that you have bestowed upon me? How much more I think of you now when that care is taken away! And so I love the whole family; never will I again find so loving a circle. O how I shall think of them time and again! All we can do now is to put our trust in Him who rules the winds and waves, and doeth all things well. O, pray for me! mother, father, all, that the good Lord will give me strength to withstand all the fiery darts of the wicked one. 'Father, I beseech thee that thy spirit may go with me and strengthen me in the hour of temptation and trial, and that thy young servant may become more perfect day by day, and feel after it is over that it has been a blessing to him.' I need say no more; you all know that I have the image of each one printed indelibly upon the innermost part of my heart. I praise God for such parents, and brothers, and sisters My mind is peaceful, and I am prepared to do whatever I have to do. May God protect, bless, and watch

over us all, and bring us to himself, where we shall
find rest for our weary souls!

"Your loving   "DOLPHIE."

After writing this letter, and watching the pilot
carry it away, Dolphie felt as if the last tie that
bound him to home was broken, and he must now
look forward to the end of his journey. A little
memorandum kept by him during the voyage tells
us of the weariness to the little company of the sev-
enty days' passage. He notes the changes of the
weather, the sight of a distant sail, or nearer view
of a homeward bound vessel, the daily progress of
the ship, as matters of interest in the monotonous
life which they led. We find also remarks on the
sermons preached by their fellow-voyager, Rev.
Mr. S., and the texts of the discourses preserved.
Reading these, I cannot but picture to myself the
group gathered in the little cabin on Sabbath afternoons—how different from Sabbath worship at
home! Yet "the Lord is nigh to all them that
call upon him," and the cabin of the *Volant* was
the birthplace of an immortal soul.

But what Dolph does not write George tells us:
of his daily increasing feebleness, of his patience
and fortitude, of his resignation to the Lord's

will, as well as his continued hope and cheer-fulness.

Like Mary, he possessed an indomitable will, which would not succumb to weakness; and we doubt not, had hope of his recovery faded in his own breast when it did in his companions', he would have died on Argentina's shore, or found a watery grave early in the homeward voyage.

On the first of March the vessel reached her destined port, where letters from home were already awaiting the travelers. They were most kindly received and hospitably entertained by our missionary at Buenos Ayres, Rev. Mr. Goodfellow, who interested himself as only a Christian could for the welfare of our dear boys. The following extracts are from Dolphie's two letters home:

"LOMOS STATION, BUENOS AYRES, *March* 10, 1866.

"DEAR PA AND MA: O how I love to speak those names and think of their owners, and how I praise my heavenly Father that he has blessed me with such parents. O that I had some means of expressing my love for you! God only knows how deeply I feel your past indulgence, care, and loving tenderness to me. Would to God that I might repay you in some way; I would do anything if it would only further your happiness. And O! my affection has been doubly increased by this separation, when I find myself deprived of your presence and care.

"When I look back upon my past life I see that many times I have grieved you and caused you pain and distress, that many times I have done wrong in the family toward my brothers and sisters, and have done things contrary both to the will of my parents and my God. And now, dear parents, I want you to pardon a sinful son, as I think God will, and pray that he may become a better son and brother, and a true follower of the Lamb. I trust that through the grace of God I am still pressing on in the path of righteousness. O! I feel there is nothing a man can give in exchange for religion; that is the root and foundation of all good. I ask your prayers, and I know I will have them, that I may grow in grace more and more, and that I may strive to know what is that good, and acceptable, and perfect will of God, and do it with all my strength. I suppose now that I must write about my health, and I will tell you plainly how things are. I find that the sea voyage has done me no good, owing, I think, to the tediousness of it and the bad living, so that upon landing

I found myself extremely weak, and my cough about the same. . . .

My dear parents, do not be discouraged about me from what I have written, for *I am not*. Let us trust it all to our heavenly Father; he certainly will do what is best for us. And may the good Lord protect and bless you both, and his grace be sufficient for you; and may he also bless me and watch over me that I stray not from the fold; and may he so teach us to live on earth, that when we come to depart this life we may all meet around the mercy seat. Amen.

" Your loving son, " DOLPH."

"LOMOS STATION, BUENOS AYRES, *March* 12, 1866.

" DEAR MOTHER: . . . I received your second batch of letters two days ago, (Saturday.) O how they comforted me to think I had such loving ones at home thinking about me, and I longed to fly away and be among you and show how I loved you. I want you to thank them all for writing to me, and tell them I will try to repay them when I get home. Now, dear mother, what words can I find to express my love for you? None. God alone can measure my affection. When I think of the years of trouble, and care, and anxiety you have had in training me in the right path, I feel nothing I have done or ever can do will half repay it. May God reward you, mother, and make your son one in whom you may delight, and who will honor his mother and his God. I have found since I have been away so many little evidences of your care and love; and above all, that precious letter! O how that has cheered me, you cannot tell! And, mother, if it should be the will of the Lord that I should give up this mortal body, I am sure enough good has resulted from my sickness to recompense for all the pain and sorrow. Mother, pray for me that ' whether living or dying I may be wholly the Lord's.'

"God grant, dear mother, that we may meet on earth; if not, in heaven. Heaven bless you, mother. "DOLPH."

As soon as they reached Buenos Ayres the boyʙ consulted an experienced physician as to the expediency of remaining there, who at once decided that they should stay no longer than was necessary to make arrangements for their immediate return. It was after seeing this physician and hearing his opinion that Dolphie wrote those lines in his first letter: "Dear parents, do not be discouraged
16

about me from what I have written, for *I am not.*
Let us trust it all to our heavenly Father ; he certainly will do what is best for us."

During their sojourn in Buenos Ayres of twenty-
eight days, Dolph endeared himself to all whose
acquaintance he made; and many remarked his
patient, uncomplaining spirit, and cheerful acquies-
cence in all the plans proposed by friends there
for his homeward voyage. In a letter written to
his father, the Rev. Mr. Goodfellow, Superintendent of the Mission, speaks thus: " Your son is
thoughtful, intelligently pious, and habitually believing; he wins favor everywhere. We shall long
remember the frail youth, and his companion of
woman-like tenderness. They did us all good, and
we regretted being of so little service to them."

On the 28th of March the young voyagers em-
barked on the " Lizzie " for Boston; Dolph full of
hopeful anticipations, George with fear and trembling lest on the homeward voyage " one should
be taken and the other left." Our kind friends in
South America, after making every arrangement
for the travelers, and bidding them " Godspeed,"
ceased not to pray that favoring winds and peaceful gales would waft the little bark speedily home,
and the Lord would spare Dolphie to reach his

father's arms, and rest his weary head upon his mother's bosom.

During the voyage his sufferings were much alleviated by the kind attention of the Christian captain, and of the passengers, two in number, who rendered him every service that sympathizing hearts could suggest and willing hands bestow. May the Lord reward them!

From letters written by these two gentlemen, we see how his life impressed them, and we cannot but be thankful that he let his light so shine:

"During his illness he never complained; was always cheerful and willing to enter into conversation, more especially about home, or a religious topic. Even when confined to his berth, the hope of seeing his friends never flagged.

"Adolphus was so submissive and patient we could but love him, and strive to prevent unnecessary suffering during the voyage. I think he had a natural desire to live; but I believe that he was well aware of his situation, and though not inclined to speak of death, his thoughtfulness and daily walk were such that I have no doubt he was aware what must be the final result of his disease. He spoke of his sickness with calmness and without a murmur, and frequently alluded to his departed sister, and spoke of the lovely Sabbath morn on which she died. The little Testament which had been her's was his pocket companion, and he would ponder the passages which she had marked, making it his daily study even when his bodily strength was nearly exhausted. I have seen him kneeling in silent prayer when he had hardly strength to rise again. I enjoyed reading the Bible and hymns to him, and though he commented but little, his sincere 'thank you' expressed not only gratitude to me, but to the Giver of the precious truths. 'Christ the good shepherd' (John x, 1–18) was one of his selections, and the ninth verse he loved much. The last time I read to him was the night preceding the one on which he died, Psalm cxix, and hymn 'Rock of Ages.' In conclusion, I can only say he died as he had lived; nay, rather, 'he is not dead, but sleepeth.'"

His hope and courage never left him; and even when, four days before reaching port, he was obliged to keep his berth from weakness, he calmly consulted George as to the best way of journeying homeward from Boston, and spoke of his joy at the thoughts of seeing home and friends once more.

It was on Friday, May 11, that he was compelled to retire to his bed, and growing gradually weaker,

George asked him, 'Dolph, if anything should happen that you should not see your parents, or that I should get home first, is there any message you would like me to take?' He immediately answered, 'Tell ma and pa I have tried to serve the Lord.' From this time his mind wandered; all his talk was of home and its dear ones, continually fancying himself among them. The last Scripture he heard was Psalm xxiii. Did he remember that Mary said those words while *she* was dying?

George had been reading, and when he stopped, Dolph whispered "read more; read the twenty-third Psalm." And I think none of that little company who gathered round his dying bed will ever forget that scene, when in sorrow and silence, broken only by the rattling of the ropes overhead and the dashing of the billows against the ship's side, they listened to those comforting words, "The Lord is my shepherd, I shall not want."

Finally, on Wednesday morning at daybreak, within thirty hours of Boston, his sufferings ended; his pure spirit returned to God who gave it.

One week before, we had received a telegram saying the "Lizzie" was outside Boston harbor, and Dolphie's parents had hastened to meet their loved boy. But after an anxious, weary week of waiting and praying, they learned it was not to be; they could never press him to their hearts again— he had *already* found rest at home.

How different was the arrival of the ship and the home-coming to what we had anticipated! Sadly the parents returned, bearing with them the lifeless body of him they loved so well; and while driving slowly up the hill to Ashridge in company with the bier that carried his precious remains, I heard for the first how Dolphie had left home with another purpose linked with his hope of recovery. He said to his mother the day before he left her, "I am determined to make a conquest of George. The Lord helping me, he shall come home a Christian." Nobly was his resolve taken, and most nobly was it carried out; and now to the love I bore for Mary is added my indebtedness to her brother, whom the Lord has already rewarded.

Adolphus died on the anniversary of Mary's funeral, and on just such another lovely day we laid him by her side, to wait the "resurrection of the just." "They were lovely and pleasant in their lives, and in their deaths they were not divided."

The following lines in memory of Adolphus were written by J. C. Johnston, Esq.:

"THE SEA GAVE UP HER DEAD."

He died upon the sea, and yet the caves
  Of ocean did not claim him for their own:
No fathomless abyss received his form;
  He sleeps not there, uncoffined and alone.

The winds that once were rude to Dolph forbore
  To buffet him, returning home to die;
At morn and eve they moaned too late, too late!
  And bore away to heaven his latest sigh.

Not for his ears the moaning of the sea
  So near to land, perhaps he felt its breath
Borne on the air; the wanderer's sweetest scent,
  Yearning for home, upon the brink of death.

And as his young heart tenderly held on
  To life, until all consciousness was past,
God made transition all the easier
  To the afflicted sufferer at last.

Death crept not unawares on Dolph; his soul,
  Firm on its anchorage, rode safely through
The only storm that strained its well-forged chain;
  The heaven beyond lay open to his view.

Lovely in his young life, he passed away,
  As the young die, dear to their God and ours,
Without a trust misplaced, or grief to cast
  Long shadows o'er a pathway strewed with flowers.

Tears have been shed for him unsparingly,
  Who never until now caused tears to flow:
Death, the revealer, shows how great our loss,
  His gain, may we who mourn together know.

The following tribute to the memory of Adolphus was prepared for the columns of "The Republican" newspaper by its editor, and printed therein, June 7, 1866:

"Death cannot come
To him untimely who is fit to die;
The less of this cold world the more of heaven;
The briefer life, the earlier immortality."—MILMAN.

"G. ADOLPHUS NORTH six months ago was one in our midst, mingling in society, having place in the Church, and a chair in the family circle of a beloved home.

"To-day we miss him in the social gathering; and his place is vacant in church, Sabbath-school, and home. The eye that so lately sparkled with delight is closed in death; the tongue that uttered so many kindly words is silent now; the hand that grasped so friendly the hand of friend is cold and rigid; the heart that beat responsive to every fellow-feeling and throbbed with holy love is still; we shall never listen to his coming footsteps again; the youthful form we so much loved lies quietly sleeping in the grave. No child ever rested more peacefully upon its mother's breast than Adolphus upon the bosom of mother earth.

"We first became acquainted with young North in the summer of 1863; and though we saw but little of him then, that little made such a favorable impression upon our minds that we were led to cultivate a more intimate acquaintance, and soon learned to love him as a brother. His unpretending manners and childlike simplicity; his genial disposition and kindness of heart; his youthful piety 'and filial affection, lent such a charm to his naturally amiable character that—to slightly alter Halleck's beautiful couplet—

'None knew him but to love him—
None named him but to praise.'

"There was little of incident in the brief young life of Adolphus North; but now that he is gone from us we treasure up with a miser's care every memento of his dear name.

"He spent an evening with the writer a few days before the vessel sailed. He was in good spirits, hopeful, and playfully remarked what he was going to bring back to some of us. We received a kind letter of thanks from him just before he left, full of tenderness and affection.

"On the 10th of December he visited the Bible class, of which he had been a member for over two years, for the last time. Adolphus had so endeared himself to his teacher, and to every member of the class, by his modest demeanor and lively interest in the lessson, answering promptly, and questioning often on difficult passages, that this last interview* was a solemn one. The prayers of the class were pledged to follow him."

The departure and return have been already described, so that the writer's beautiful recital need not be inserted.

"On Saturday, the 19th of May, his funeral took place at his father's residence. There was a large concourse of citizens, friends, and relatives present; and among them the Bible class, of which he had been a member, who sincerely and deeply mourned their loss. His pall-bearers were selected from among their number. Addresses were made by Rev. J. P. Hermance, of the Methodist Episcopal Church, Sing Sing, and Revs. R. S. Foster and A. C. Foss, of New York. The following hymn, composed for the occasion by the teacher of the Bible class, was effectively sung, joined in by all present:

FUNERAL HYMN.

O! holy Father! unto thee
We bow, submissive to thy will,
And own, in deep humility,
That thou alone this void can fill.

'We come to lay the casket by
    That held the jewel of our love;
In the cold grave it there shall lie—
    The jewel in a crown above!

'Tis meet when spring with opening flowers
    Bedecks the earth in beauty rare,
The young, the loved, the lost of ours,
    Should bloom in heaven—perennial there!

O God! could we but lift the vail
    That hides eternity from view,
We would no more our lost bewail,
    No more our tears would we renew;

For high o'er yon empyreal plains
    Angels and spirits of the blest
Are welcoming, in unknown strains,
    ADOLPHUS to the realms of rest.

Then cease these sorrows, cease these tears;
    To God be all the glory given;
A few more fleeting days and years,
    And we shall meet again—in heaven!

"After the funeral rites were performed his remains were taken and deposited in the Sleepy Hollow Cemetery, at Tarrytown, there to rest in 'sure and certain hope of a glorious resurrection.'

"Wishing further to impress upon the young the beautiful example of Adolphus, the Rev. Mr. Hermance preached an able memorial discourse on his life and death in the Methodist Episcopal Church of Sing Sing, Sabbath evening, June 3, and

the following estimation of his character is taken
from that discourse. He took for the foundation
of his remarks this text: 'Leaving us an example,
that ye should follow his steps.' 1 Peter ii, 21.

" He was a kind, gentle, polite young man. It
is saying no more than the facts will warrant that,
during the latter years of his life, no one ever
heard him speak an angry word; no one ever witnessed in him any rudeness, or saw him do an unkind act. Adolphus won himself friends wherever
he went. Such was the uniform politeness which
marked his intercourse with others in every place
—such was the sweetness of his disposition, and
the gentleness of his manners, that those who came
in contact with and knew him intimately, felt not
only admiration, but love for him.

" Of his intellectual endowments it is only necessary for me to say that they were such as to lead
to the brightest hopes for his future position in life.
He was certainly possessed of mental capacities
which, with his habits of attentive inquiry and discipline, would have fitted him for usefulness, and
an honorable place among his fellows. During the
year 1865, at the request of the committee on
speakers, he delivered an address before the Juve-
nile Missionary Society of this Church. This was

a happy effort for one so young, and will be long remembered by all who heard it.

"As we turn to the contemplation of his religious character, we shall discover that which is equally worthy of our approbation. He was, on the day of his departure to the haven of the good, seventeen years and ten months of age. About seven or eight years of that life were passed away by him in the service of God. It will thus be seen that his conversion took place at the early age of between nine and ten. That his conversion was genuine and thorough, is proven by the fact that though aforetime he was no more obedient, truthful, or gentle, or lovely than other children, yet, after this important event in his life, he became changed in a marked manner.

"On the 8th of November, 1863, he became a member of the Bible class connected with this Church, and under the instruction of our beloved Brother Sheldon. Here his attendance at his class, his thoroughness in preparation, his attention to the instruction of his teacher, and the propriety of his general deportment, soon won for him a place in the hearts of his teacher and all his classmates. And these favorable impressions, produced at the time of his entrance into the class, were intensified and deepened by all his subsequent course. The impressions made upon the mind of his Bible class teacher as to his religious life were decidedly favorable—that his experience was thorough, deep, and pure.

"The beautiful letter written on his seventeenth birthday shows how his spirit was yearning after the invisible things of God; how former disobedience and forgetfulness were rendered hateful as the clearer lights of a deeper experience threw their illuminating rays upon the past of his life; how God was refining the gold and polishing the diamond, which was, ere many months had passed, to be set as a signet in his Redeemer's crown.

"His life has not been in vain. Far, far from it. We are all of us the better for his bright example —his beautiful life. His name and memory are 'like precious ointment poured forth.' His image is as the memory of a beautiful picture which men love to dwell upon in thoughtful delight. The aroma of his chastened spirit, and the fragrance of his beautiful Christian life, yet linger along the paths he trod, and fill the places he frequented. They linger in the rooms of his father's house; they hover over the group gathering Sabbath after Sabbath in the Bible class room; they float along the dusty thoroughfares he used to travel; they linger around the Sunday-school in the Scarborough school-house; they are in the atmosphere of the school-rooms where he studied; they are hanging like a felt presence over the decks of the *Volante* and the *Lizzie*, and are penetrating their cabins; they are belting the shores of the South American coast, and are felt in the mission station of Buenos Ayres; and, penetrating the sensibilities of those who surrounded him in the moments of greatest trial, they have diffused themselves into distant regions, laden with priceless benedictions. Earth has been made happier, human lives have been made purer, and heaven has been made dearer, by the life and death of G. Adolphus North."

The following letter to his father has just come to hand. The writer, Rev. J. W. Shank, is a missionary to Buenos Ayres, and went out in company with the subject of this sketch.

"BUENOS AYRES, S. A., *August* 20, 1866.

" DEAR BROTHER: On the 10th ultimo Brother Goodfellow received a letter conveying intelligence of your bereavement in the death of your son Adolphus. Great as must have been the shock to you, I believe that mine was only second to it; the more so, because I had prayed that his fond hopes and wishes might be realized in once more seeing loved ones so dear to his heart. When the news came I was about leaving for the camp, and could not write; but since my return, though at so late an hour, I wish to express my sympathies, hoping they may add something to the preciousness of your memory of one so dear.

" Firstly, he was a Christian. Of this he convinced all who knew him. He used to lead us in our devotions until his cough became too severe. The captain frequently remarked to me, how much he enjoyed his prayers, and as often said he believed that if there was a Christian on earth Adolphus was one. George also said to me one day when we were talking of his illness, " One thing is certain, if Adolphus dies he will go to heaven." This was before George had become a Christian, but while he was seriously meditating upon the matter. There is no doubt but that the conduct of Adolphus had much to do with George's decision. So may we not hope that, though you were to see your son no more, God had sent him away to win a soul to Christ, and gain a star for his heavenly crown.

" Secondly, he was a lover of knowledge; his attainments had already made him in some respects the superior of all on board our vessel. Often did we sit and hear him relate the contents of a volume he had read, or some anecdote, or give a description of some beautiful scenery which he had witnessed. He read as much as he was able, but longed especially for the knowledge of a collegiate, and for European travel, yet seemed perfectly to resign all these into the hands of Him whom he served.

" Thirdly, he was amiable. Wherever he went, his graceful manners, pleasant countenance, and fine social qualities begat him friends upon the slightest acquaintance. For social abilities he was rarely equaled by any of his age.

" But all these things *you* know better than I ; and you feel his loss. The distress of your not being permitted to see him is only equaled by his not being permitted to see you. He often spoke of all the family with tenderest feelings, and said that if he ever should reach home again, he would know how to realize parental and brotherly affection, for which he felt that he had formerly been too ungrateful. He carried " *home* " in his mind, as a paradise second only to heaven, and his delight was to let his memory linger around the family circle, while his lips expressed to us the joys and pleasures of a happy family.

" But now he is gone, yet perchance his spirit lingers. He beckons heavenward; and while there is another tie in heaven, may the " Comforter" dwell in the hearts of a bereaved family."

THE GRAVES OF MARY AND ADOLPHUS IN SLEEPY HOLLOW CEMETERY

BY THEIR FATHER.

A CLASSIC vale lay sleeping by,
　Renowned through Irving's matchless pen;
While Hudson rolled its waters nigh,
　And sent its tides to sea again.

Between the vale and river lay
　A burial ground of beauty rare;
Where tree, and mound, and winding way,
　All blending, make the prospect fair.

A shady spot we chose—a dell
　Hid from the gaze of vulgar eyes;
Where parted ones might safely dwell
　Until the trump shall bid them rise.

A score of years and more had flown
　Since we were joined in holy love;
And plants had round our table grown,
　Nourished by Him who dwells above.

A peaceful group without a foe,
　No turf we broke in all those years;
Yet sighing said, There's coming woe;
　This joy's too long—'twill turn to tears.

Death loves a shining mark, and she
　Was chosen first—fair as the moon.
Darling Mary!—'tis God's decree—
　Must lead the way to the grave's dark gloom.

17

Our first-born—loving, wise, and good—
  Bade fair for lengthened years; so strong,
So healthful, 'mid the fairest stood,
  E'en though a thousand swelled the throng.

But health and beauty were not shields
  Against the fearful shafts of death;
She in the painful contest yields,
  Yet triumphs in her latest breath.

We laid her down in Greenwood's shades,
  Nor murmured, since her spirit bright
Had gone where pleasure never fades,
  To wear her robe of spotless white.

A son we had of precious worth;
  All spake of him in words of praise;
His name like ointment when poured forth,
  And all his paths were pleasant ways.

One morn he rose with pallid brow;
  The luster from his eye had fled;
A cough, dread sound, we hear it now;
  Alarm and sorrow o'er us spread.

In haste we sent him on the deep,
  To far off Argentina's shore,
With prayer that God our boy would keep,
  And bring him safely home once more.

Four months he tossed upon the sea,
  But weaker grew each passing day,
Till off New England's rocky lea
  His spirit flew the heavenly way.

Anchored in Boston's peaceful bay,
　We hailed the bark that brought our boy;
There, coffined, dear Adolphus lay;
　We kissed his brow with tearful joy,

Thankful his precious face to see;
　That, nursed by friendly brawny hands,
He was not cast into the sea,
　Nor left to die in distant lands.

So from New England's rocky shore,
　From Greenwood's quiet hill-side shade,
With tender care their dust we bore,
　And side by side the dear ones laid.

Here the pure marble speaks their worth,
　And tells, in simple chiseled words,
Their length of days, their death, their birth,
　And how at last they are the Lord's.

And oft the stricken family meet
　With tears and flowers around their mounds,
And pledge the solemn vow to greet
　Their Early Crowned where bliss abounds.

DOLPHIE'S FRIEND.

THE reader of the foregoing memoir of Adolphus North must have observed with melancholy interest the occasional allusions to the companion of his last journey.

George, like Adolphus, was smitten with pulmonary disease, and sought with him a more genial clime. But, unlike Adolphus, he was not a Christian. Trained by Christian parents, grown up from infancy to youth under the influence of the Sunday-school and Church, and exhibiting a correct outward deportment, his heart was still far from God. Because of Adolphus's decided Christian character he was at first averse to the contemplated companionship. Happily Adolphus's influence on the voyage not only secured to himself his affection, but at last led him to Christ; so that on their arrival at Buenos Ayres George manifested his new resolutions by kneeling at the sacramental altar the first Sabbath after reaching that distant city. During the short sojourn in the Argentine Republic George's

attentions to his feeble friend were no less tender
than constant. But it was on shipboard, on the
return voyage, that his devotion to his dying companion was womanly in its fidelity and ceaseless
care. The officers of the vessel relate how the robust youth sat beside the invalid, as on sunny days
he reclined on the deck, and read to him the precious words of Jesus; and how he also sat patiently and long beside the narrow berth, from
which the dying friend was no more to rise, ministering to his wants with a sister's tenderness.
Landing at Boston, he saw the body of his comrade placed safely in charge of the waiting parents
and then hastened to New York, where a happy
family group hailed with joy his return. Ah, the
different emotions which pervaded the two family
circles! "One had been taken and the other left."
George appeared to be quite restored to health,
but this was delusive, for in another season his old
symptoms returned. We watched with painful
solicitude the pale cheek, the lusterless eye, and the
hesitating walk, which betokened the certainty of
his early fall. A summer passed, and then a bleak
winter, and another summer came. He had now
become greatly enfeebled. As a last resort, and
mainly because of his own desire, his mother ac-

companied him to Chicago, on their way to the
healthful air of Minnesota. But physician and
friends forbade further prosecution of their plan,
and advised an immediate return to New York.
Accordingly the mother with the frail sufferer entered the cars for their long, sad journey. During the
day George sat or reclined in quietness and silence,
giving evidence of weakness but not of pain. Not-
withstanding his feebleness he was observed to
read his pocket Testament most of the weary
hours. Occupying a sleeping-car, his mother laid
him down gently to sleep as if he were an infant
again. Undisturbed, he slumbered on until nearly
midnight; then awaking, his pillow was read-
justed, after which he declared his feeling of
comfort and slept again. This time it was that
sleep that knows no waking. The vigilant mother,
in the silence of midnight listened, but the weary
wheels of life stood still. Six hours more and he
might have died in the midst of his family; but no,
he was to imitate the closing hours of his departed
comrade, and reach the heavenly before the earthly
home. He returned from Buenos Ayres a Christian,
and united with the Church. For a season there
was a pause in his religious growth; then again
his covenants were renewed. As he grew feeble

there came a soft, resigned expression in his face, and a subdued cheerfulness in the tones of his voice that rendered his society pleasant, and assured him a welcome in the families where he visited. As he declined in health his spirituality increased, and thus the evidences were constantly developed of his ripeness for heaven.

And so at last these fellow-voyagers have reached the end of their pilgrimage, and have exchanged greetings in a world without pain or sorrow.

BOOKS FOR SUNDAY-SCHOOLS.

200 Mulberry-street, New York.

THE LOCAL PREACHER;

Or, the Trial of Faith. Reminiscences of the West
India Islands. Second Series, No. III. Three Illustrations. 18mo., pp. 135.

THE RODEN FAMILY;

Or, the Sad End of Bad Ways. Reminiscences of the
West India Islands. Second Series, No. II. Three
Illustrations. 18mo., pp. 159.

RELIGIOUS ANECDOTES

And Moral Lessons for Sabbath-School Scholars. By
G. D. CHENOWETH. 18mo., pp. 110.

THE IRISH SCHOLAR;

Or, Popery and Protestant Christianity. A Narrative.
By Rev. T. W. AVELING. Three Illustrations. 18mo.,
pp. 175.

ANNIE WALTON.

A Tale from Real Life. Three Illustrations. 18mo.,
pp. 119.

VILLAGE SCIENCE;

Or, the Laws of Nature explained. By the Author
of "Peeps at Nature," "Nature's Wonders," etc. With
Illustrations. 18mo., pp. 285.

THE DYING HOURS

Of Good and Bad Men contrasted. 18mo., pp. 150.

THE CHINESE;

Or, Conversations on the Country and People of China.
Illustrated. 18mo., pp. 144.

LEARNING TO FEEL.

Illustrated. Two volumes, 18mo., pp. 298.

LEARNING TO ACT.

Three Illustrations. 18mo., pp. 144.

BOOKS FOR SUNDAY-SCHOOLS.

200 Mulberry-street, New York.

WAYSIDE FRAGMENTS;
Or, Wonders in Common Things. By the Author of "Peeps at Nature," "Nature's Wonders," "Village Science," etc. Twelve Illustrations. 18mo., pp. 204.

LIFE OF REV. ENOCH GEORGE,
One of the Bishops of the M. E. Church. By Benjamin St. James Fry. 18mo., pp. 124.

LIFE OF JOHN BUNYAN,
Author of "The Pilgrim's Progress." By Stephen B. Wickens. Six Illustrations. 18mo., pp. 336.

THOMAS HAWKEY TREFFRY:
Parental Portraiture of Thomas Hawkey Treffry, who died at Falmouth, April 19, 1821, aged eighteen years. By Rev. Richard Treffry. 18mo., pp. 171.

ANCIENT EGYPT:
Its Monuments and History. Three Illustrations. 18mo., pp. 214.

MEMOIR OF OLD HUMPHREY:
With Gleanings from his Portfolio, in Prose and Verse. Two Illustrations. 18mo., pp. 298.

THE PROMPTER;
Or, the Sunday-Scholar's True Friend. Two volumes, 18mo., each, pp. 288.

ISABEL;
Or, Influence for Good: with Examples. Three Illustrations. 18mo., pp. 176.

THE TWO DOVES;
Or, Memoirs of Margaret and Anna Dove, late of Leeds, England. By Peter M'Owan. 18mo., pp. 88.

THE CONVERTED JEWESS:
A Memoir of Maria ——. 18mo., pp. 107.

BOOKS FOR SUNDAY-SCHOOLS.

200 Mulberry-street, New York.

NAPOLEON BONAPARTE.
Sketches from the History of Napoleon Bonaparte. Written for the Young. Six Illustrations. 18mo., pp. 126.

THE TEMPTATION;
Or, Henry Thornton. Showing the Progress and Fruits of Intemperance. Three Illustrations. 18mo., pp. 90.

HARRIET GRAY;
Or, the Selfish Girl cured. 18mo., pp. 80.

THE LIVES OF THE CESARS.
For Week-day Reading. Six Illustrations. 18mo., pp. 221.

BE GOOD:
An Important Precept Illustrated in Ralph's Account of a Visit to the Country. Four Illustrations. 18mo., pp. 60.

HADASSAH;
Or, the Adopted Child. Two Illustrations. 18mo., pp. 112.

CUBA.
By Rev. JAMES RAWSON, A.M. Illustrated. 18mo., pp. 70.

THE MISSIONARY TEACHER:
A Memoir of Cyrus Shepard, embracing a Brief Sketch of the Early History of the Oregon Mission. By Rev. Z. A. MUDGE. Seven Illustrations. 18mo., pp. 221.

CHEERFUL CHAPTERS:
Adapted to Youth, and not unsuited to Age. By old ALAN GRAY. Four Illustrations. 18mo., pp. 179.

DENNIS BROOKS;
Or, a Mother's Grief. 18mo., pp. 62.

BOOKS FOR SUNDAY-SCHOOLS.

200 Mulberry-street, New York.

LIFE OF REV. RICHARD WATSON,

Author of Theological Institutes, Dictionary, Exposition of the Gospels, etc. By STEPHEN B. WICKENS. 18mo., pp. 262.

SENIOR CLASSES IN SUNDAY-SCHOOLS.

Containing Cooper's Prize Essay, and other Treatises on the Subject. 18mo., pp. 203.

PARIS: ANCIENT AND MODERN.

18mo., pp. 212.

THREE MONTHS UNDER THE SNOW.

The Journal of a Young Inhabitant of the Jura. Translated from the French of J. J. PORCHAT. Four Illustrations. 18mo., pp. 178.

THREE DAYS ON THE OHIO RIVER.

By FATHER WILLIAM. Two Illustrations. 18mo., pp. 60.

ORIGIN AND PROGRESS OF LANGUAGE.

18mo., pp. 227.

THE LAMP AND THE LANTERN;

Or, Light for the Tent and the Traveler. By JAMES HAMILTON, D.D. 18mo., pp. 202.

LIFE OF ALEXANDER THE GREAT.

18mo., pp. 208.

MY SABBATH-SCHOOL SCHOLARS.

Recollections of my Sabbath-School Scholars. By a Minister of the Gospel. 18mo., pp. 70.

THE BIBLE IN MANY TONGUES.

18mo., pp. 216.

REMARKABLE ESCAPES FROM PERIL.

18mo., pp. 171.

BOOKS FOR SUNDAY-SCHOOLS.

200 Mulberry-street, New York.

MARGARET CRAVEN;

Or, Beauty of the Heart. By the Author of "The Lost Key," "The Golden Mushroom," and "The Little Water-cress Sellers." Five Illustrations. 18mo., pp. 175.

ELLINOR GREY:

Or, the Sunday-School Class at Trimble Hollow. By Mrs. H. C. GARDNER, Author of "Annie Lee," etc. Four Illustrations. 18mo., pp. 195.

AUNT EFFIE;

Or, the Pious Widow and her Infidel Brother. By Rev. DANIEL WISE, Author of "Guide to the Saviour," "Path of Life," "Young Man's Counselor," etc. Two Illustrations. 18mo., pp. 174.

MINNIE RAY:

A Story of Faith and Good Works. By Mrs. C. M. EDWARDS, Author of "The Herbert Family," "The Itinerant," etc. Four Illustrations. 18mo., pp. 198.

SARAH NEAL.

A Tale of Real Life. By the Author of "Roland Rand" and "The Homely Child." Three Illustrations. 18mo., pp. 76.

BE COURTEOUS;

Or, Religion the True Refiner. By Mrs. M. H. MAXWELL. Three Illustrations. 18mo., pp. 183.

A SCHOOL-BOY'S LIFE:

Being a Memoir of John Lang Bickersteth, late of Rugby School. 18mo., pp. 69.

THE VISITOR;

Or, Calls of Usefulness. Illustrated. Two volumes, 18mo., pp. 105, 94.

LEARNING TO THINK.

Illustrated. Two volumes, 18mo., pp. 135, 144.

BOOKS FOR SUNDAY-SCHOOLS.

200 Mulberry-street, New York.

THE WILMOT FAMILY;

Or, Children at Home. A Picture of Real Life. From the second London edition. Five Illustrations. 18mo., pp. 314.

TOO LATE!

Or, the Fatal Effects of Procrastination. Illustrated in a Series of Authentic Sketches. By Rev. J. T. BARR, A.M., Author of "Recollections of a Minister," etc., etc. 18mo., pp. 115.

THE FOSTER BROTHERS;

Or, Duty To-day and Pleasure To-morrow: A Story for Boys. 18mo., pp. 138.

THE MARTYRS OF BOHEMIA;

Or, Brief Memoirs of John Huss and Jerome of Prague. 18mo., pp. 237.

THE GOLDEN CITY:

With a Sketch of a Family on its Way thither. Two Illustrations. 18mo., pp. 94.

THE SOLAR SYSTEM.

Illustrated. Two volumes, 18mo., pp. 442.

THE SHIPWRECK;

Or, a Summer Scene and Winter Story. Two Illustrations. 18mo., pp. 109.

CHRISTIAN JOY;

Or, the Second Fruit of the Spirit. Illustrated in an Epistolary Narrative. 18mo., pp. 87.

THE BRANDY DROPS;

Or, Charlie's Pledge. A Temperance Story. By AUNT JULIA. 18mo., pp. 103.

LEARNING TO CONVERSE.

Illustrated. 18mo., pp. 134.

BOOKS FOR SUNDAY-SCHOOLS.

200 Mulberry-street, New York.

FRANK HARRISON:
The History of a Wayward Boy. Three Illustrations.
18mo., pp. 150.

THE CHECKERED SCENE;
Or, Memorials of Samuel Oliver. By Rev. GERVASE
SMITH. 18mo., pp. 168.

CHILDREN OF THE BIBLE.
Eleven Illustrations. 18mo., pp. 122.

NATURE'S WONDERS;
Or, God's Care over all his Works. By the Author of
"Peeps at Nature." Illustrated. 18mo., pp. 226.

LITTLE JAMES;
Or, the Story of a Good Boy's Life and Death. John
Reinhard Hedinguer; or, the Faithful Chaplain: being
an Account of an Extraordinarily Pious and Devoted
Minister of Christ. 18mo., pp. 54.

THE HAPPY RESOLVE.
A Tale from Real Life. 18mo., pp. 78.

SERIOUS ADVICE
From a Father to his Children. Recommended to
Parents, Guardians, Governors of Seminaries, and to
Teachers of Sunday-Schools. By CHARLES ATMORE.
18mo., pp. 32.

MONEY:
Its Nature, History, Uses, and Responsibilities. 18mo.,
pp. 208.

FOOTPRINTS OF POPERY;
Or, Places where Martyrs have Suffered. Seven Illustrations. 18mo., pp. 200.

BABYLON
And the Banks of the Euphrates. 18mo., pp. 211.

BOOKS FOR SUNDAY-SCHOOLS.

200 Mulberry-street, New York.

VOICES FROM THE OLD ELM;

Or, Uncle Henry's Talks with the Little Folks. By Rev. H. P. ANDREWS, Author of "Six Steps to Honor." 18mo., pp. 277.

BECHUANAS OF SOUTH AFRICA.

Mr. Moffat and the Bechuanas of South Africa. Three Illustrations. 18mo., pp. 111.

THE EMIGRANT BOY AND HIS SISTER.

By the Author of "Little Ella." Seven Illustrations. 18mo., pp. 217.

IMOGEN, THE ORPHAN PRINCESS.

A Story of the Times in which the Gospel was first preached in England. Three Illustrations. 18mo., pp. 119.

THE STRANGE PLANET,

And other Allegories. With Illustrations. 18mo., pp. 117.

THE YOUNG ENVELOPE-MAKERS.

By the Author of "Matty Gregg," "Margaret Craven," "The Lost Key," etc., etc. Five Illustrations. 18mo., pp. 198.

STATE AND PROSPECTS OF CHINA.

Medhurst's State and Prospects of China. Five Illustrations. 18mo., pp. 272.

AUNT CLARA'S STORIES FOR HER NEPHEWS.

Four Illustrations. 18mo., pp. 102.

OLD ANTHONY'S HINTS TO YOUNG PEOPLE,

To make them both Cheerful and Wise. Five Illustrations. 18mo., pp. 166.

EPHRAIM HOLDING'S HOMELY HINTS

To Sunday-School Teachers. 18mo., pp. 213.